THE MERMAN KING

LORDS OF THE ABYSS

MICHELLE M. PILLOW

MICHELLE M. PILLOW® - MICHELLEPILLOW.COM

ABOUT THE MERMAN KING
PARANORMAL UNDERWATER
SHAPESHIFTER ROMANCE

Lucius, King of the Mermen, and ruler of the city of Atlantes, shoulders the guilt for his people's curse. After being trapped under the sea for two millennia, the time has come for his people to possibly surface and breathe air. He's ready to be the first to test the theory, but things do not go as expected when a captivating beauty seemingly falls into his lap—and his ocean.

Is Olivette a present from the gods, or a warning to stay punished beneath the waves where his people belong?

LORDS OF THE ABYSS SERIES

The Mighty Hunter
Commanding the Tides
Captive of the Deep
Surrender to the Sea
Making Waves
The Merman King

Dragon Lords Series

Barbarian Prince

Perfect Prince

Dark Prince

Warrior Prince

His Highness The Duke

The Stubborn Lord

The Reluctant Lord

The Impatient Lord

The Dragon's Queen

Lords of the Var® Series

The Savage King

The Playful Prince
The Bound Prince
The Rogue Prince
The Pirate Prince

Captured by a Dragon-Shifter Series
Determined Prince
Rebellious Prince
Stranded with the Cajun
Hunted by the Dragon
Mischievous Prince
Headstrong Prince

Space Lords Series
His Frost Maiden
His Fire Maiden
His Metal Maiden
His Earth Maiden
His Woodland Maiden

Dynasty Lords Series

Seduction of the Phoenix
Temptation of the Butterfly

To learn more about the Qurilixen World series of books and to stay up to date on the latest book list visit www.MichellePillow.com

AUTHOR UPDATES

To stay informed about when a new book in the series installments is released, sign up for updates:

michellepillow.com/author-updates

1

Olivette Waller smiled even though she was dressed up like a slutty Mrs. Santa Claus, complete with black fishnet stockings, glitter lipstick, and a tinsel hairpiece that gave the impression she'd made out with a Christmas tree. Though, she supposed that was better than the woman dressed like an Easter bunny who'd fallen on hard times, or the leprechaun who wore more green body paint than clothes, or the Thanksgiving turkey lady with a feather duster attached to her butt.

The party planner who'd hired her clearly hadn't thought how ill-conceived it was to wear high heels on a yacht in open water while carrying a tray of champagne flutes. Then again, maybe he just didn't care. Patrick's Party Events wasn't exactly known for tastefulness. He had, after all, planned a party at sea with the theme of Every U.S. Holiday.

Her legs ached. The breeze from the ocean caused her to shiver whenever she made her rounds along the deck. The red material of the costume felt like a wool blend and had become itchy, with the added bonus of feathery white bits of fluff that stuck to her thighs, neck, and arms. Had this been a simple office party, as she was told it would be, the discomfort would have ended with the clothes.

Olivette had the impression only part of the office was invited—the rich, bloated, drunken, handsy part. But, what was a girl to do? The economy tanked and so did her flower shop. People didn't need bouquets when they were struggling to pay mortgages and buy groceries. Her contribution to the farmers' market helped, but it wasn't enough to keep her afloat.

"There's my little ho ho ho."

Olivette flinched. She'd tried to avoid Tanner Tapert for the last two hours. His breath reeked of bourbon and cigars. He claimed to be the aide of some politician he wasn't at liberty to name. She believed it. He had the expensive suit and smarmy appeal of someone in politics.

"What do you say we go jingle some bells?"

Tanner gave a hearty laugh as he continued his barrage of holiday-themed come-on lines. He'd offered to let her unwrap his present, light his Yule log, and an inventive yet highly inappropriate suggestion involving elves, a tree, and a three-way. She knew he was more interested in showing off for his friends than he had any real attraction for her. Olivette could have been anyone.

Still laughing, he managed to add, "I'll give you a ride on my one horse open sleigh."

Olivette arched a brow and swiped his empty glass from the edge of the boat. She couldn't help herself as she gave him a dismissive once over. "One horse? I'm sorry, I like my rides to have a little more horsepower under the hood."

Tanner's expression fell.

Olivette felt a small victory as the man's cronies laughed at his expense. If he complained, Patrick probably wouldn't hire her back. Glancing at her attire, she couldn't say she'd be too bothered by that. There had to be better jobs.

Only three hours left until the boat turned around and took them back to shore. She sidestepped hands that tried to make their way up her skirt as she filled her tray with discarded glasses and emptied ashtrays. The more she did now, the less she'd have to clean up when they docked. She noticed several of the waitresses taking things a little too far with the holiday cheer, dancing seductively for tips and forgetting their duties altogether as they partook of the refreshments they were supposed to be serving. The turkey had plucked a few of her feathers and used them to tickle the guests, and she'd witnessed more than a few green kiss marks on cheeks from the leprechaun.

"Two hours and fifty minutes until I get to go home," Olivette whispered, leaning against the railing to look out at the ocean. The sun was setting and she could almost forget the party behind her. Who would know if she hid for a couple of hours? Maybe staying late to clean up would be better than trying to weave through the crowd.

She found a private spot near a side rail to watch the water. The music became louder, and the laughter rose to new levels to overcome the sudden rise in volume.

Movement on the surface of the ocean caught her attention. At first, she thought it was a hand reaching up from below. Leaning forward, she squinted into the sunset. The image disappeared, and she gave a small laugh. It was probably a dolphin. No one would be swimming this far out to sea, especially not at sunset without some kind of boat nearby. The boat she was on moved in the wrong direction for it to have been anyone from their vessel.

"If it isn't Mrs. Claus, comedian."

Olivette stiffened as the smell of bourbon and cigars wafted against her cheek. She tried to pull away, but Tanner grabbed her arm. She cried out, but her scream was lost in the chaotic noise of the party. Even if they did hear her, she wasn't sure anyone would come to her aid.

2

KING LUCIUS LOWERED his tingling hand and stared at the ocean's surface from below. The scales of his blue tail would camouflage him in the water. It had been a very long time since he'd been this close to the surface world. Normally, only the elite group of hunters made their way to this border. He'd forgotten how bright the sunlight breaking through the water could be, streaming down until the darkness of the abyss below swallowed every last glimmer.

That was where he lived—below in the darkness. That was where his arrogance had condemned his people centuries ago. The thin barrier between ocean and air was so fragile, and yet it held them down in their place.

Since the beginning there had been one sure way to die as Merr—break the surface. If Merr skin were to touch surface air, it'd burn. If he were to breathe it into his lungs, he'd die a painful death. Until now. Today he touched air for the first time in more centuries than he could count. It was only a few seconds, but his hand returned unharmed. Would his lungs fare the same? Very little scared him, but crossing that barrier terrified him.

Lucius had much on his mind as he stared up at the surface world. The light above shifted and changed color, the white fading into orange. It had danced along his fingers as he touched it. He felt the presence of Brutus and Demon beneath him. The hunters had insisted they join him, and he allowed it only because someone needed to report back if things did not go well.

Lucius had been king a very long time, longer than any man should be made to carry the burden. Above, he'd ruled over Greece, Italy, and Egypt. His empire of Atlantes had been vast, and his ego great.

It was not meant to be.

When the god Poseidon had brought Atlantes up from the water to bless them, he had not done it so they could conquer their neighbors, or raid villages, or consume more than they needed. That decision had been Lucius'. The fault of that greed was shared with his people as they were the ones who'd demanded more. He was the one who gave it to them.

Below, he still ruled Atlantes, but it was only the small piece he was given to begin with. Because of his arrogance, Poseidon had cursed them. He waited until Lucius' soldiers were home, until they were drunk and in the prime of their blustering. And in a great and mighty show of his power, the god of the sea plucked them from the earth and cast them down as if they were a pebble to be thrown away. But no god's punishment was ever light.

Poseidon could have let them drown and made that the end of the story. Instead, he cursed them. He turned their legs to tails and ripped fins out of their forearms. He molded them into half men, half fish and held them up as a warning to everyone else who thought they were better than the gods.

As Atlantes fell, it took the light with it, a beacon that the newly turned Merr should follow. They swam after it, a clumsy effort in their new bodies. The creatures they passed were terrifying to their landlocked eyes—tentacle arms, bloated, pale bodies, and razor-sharp teeth. The protective dome covering their home was the only light in the abyss, a bonfire in the dark showing them the way back. When finally they reached the bottom, and Atlantes settled in a cloud of dust, they found themselves pressed to an invisible barrier looking in at a magical land. Some knocked to get in. Some prayed. Some cried. All stayed stuck to that dome, desperate to get inside.

A dozen brave men, including the twins Brutus and Demon, went with the king to find an entrance. They explored the dangerous caves of the base and were the first to dare to cross over into the dome. They watched their tails pull apart into human legs for the first time. He still remembered standing on dry land inside the dome, looking up at a literal sea of faces looking in.

Those initial twelve men had become hunters, the elite soldiers allowed to patrol the ocean. He split them up into four teams of three—the *Hunters*, *Knights*, *Soldiers*, and *Warriors*.

Patrolling turned into hunting down the lost who did not make it to the dome. Unfortunately, those Merr had transformed a second time, becoming water spirits they called the scylla. They were dangerous creatures, mindless, reckless, forever searching for a life they could no longer have. Or perhaps they were angry and jealous, crashing boats to drown mortals. Regardless, the hunters had spent the last millennia chasing them down and making the waters safer. The twins had lost their brother in such a way, and Demon had almost lost his new wife. Luckily, they'd managed to save Lady Victoria.

'*I have decided,*' the king said at last, knowing that the two hunters would carry out his wishes. They spoke by telepathy in the water. '*If I do not survive this, I wish for there to be no king for at least ten years. I turn over control of Atlantes to the hunters. After that time, you can decide how best to rule. The twelve of you know the ocean and politics better than any. I trust you to guide and help our people. And I trust you to deal with the Olympian cult.*'

'*You don't have to do this,*' Brutus said. The brothers were identical. Their black eyes glinted with a silver sheen. Long black hair matched their black fins and tails. Their larger size made them formidable. '*I touched the surface air and did not burn. Let me be the first to breathe.*'

'*You have a new wife. Think of Lady Laurel,*' the king dismissed. That was another reason he'd brought the twins instead of two others who did not have wives. He could use that to keep them from trying to take his place.

The king had hoped, as they all secretly

dreamed, that one day the gods would bless him with a woman, with love, with a wife. Five of his hunters had rescued wives recently. That had to mean something—five women salvaged from the surface world and brought down to Atlantes.

But how was that right? To find love, they had to curse the women and make them Merr. And now none of the wives could return to their former homes.

King Lucius was the reason Poseidon had cursed them. That made it his duty to be the first to surface and breathe the air. Well, perhaps not the first. There were rumors that his ex-lover Maia had found a way.

Maia had declared herself a queen, defected and taken several women with her, then established herself as an Olympian in an area of the Atlantean forest she called Mt. Olympus. They didn't hear from the Olympian cult for a long time. Then rumors started spreading of the mermaids going to the surface and luring human males to their death. The mermaids lured men into the ocean and captured them to be their servants. The stories were secondhand accounts but if they were true, Maia might have stumbled upon an inoculation for surface-air exposure. One of their scientists had spent time with the Olympians and he was about to test her theory.

'It doesn't have to be you,' Demon said. 'We can turn around now.'

'Lady Bridget has been making us eat that awful Olympian seaweed for years. Trust me, if it's not working to acclimatize us to the surface, I think we'd all want to know.' The king tried to make light of what he was facing.

'Maybe finding hunter wives is a way of indicating Poseidon is watching us,' Brutus said. 'Perhaps we should just turn around and wait for a sign.'

'What do you think, Demon?' Lucius swam a few feet away from the surface so he could look his friends in the eyes.

'I think you are my king and I will always follow your command,' Demon said. 'No one blames you for what happened. We all had stopped going to Poseidon's temples. The god punished all of us, not just you. You do not have to do this. The kingdom needs you. And who is to say that if we were allowed to return to the world of sunlight, we would want it? We have been under for so long, centuries upon centuries. Have we stopped to consider that perhaps we only yearn for the surface because that's what we've been thinking about since being cast down? What happens if we go up? Will we turn back? Will we begin to yearn for life in the ocean? For the isolation of

Atlantes? I don't think it's worth the risk. After so long, Atlantes is home. We have been there longer than we were on the surface. Maybe it's time to accept it. Let us go home, my king.'

'You have no sins to atone for,' Brutus asserted.

'I have always appreciated your fine council.' The king clasped his friends on their shoulders and squeezed. *'Thank you.'*

King Lucius had made up his mind. It was time.

'Surface slowly,' Brutus instructed. *'And don't stay up long.'*

'Hold your breath and let the air in slowly,' Demon added. *'And be careful, I feel vibrations on the water. There is a boat nearby.'*

King Lucius would not let the fear stop him. That he could still be afraid after so long meant something, and he held on to that emotion. He moved his tail slowly, easing his way toward the surface light. He focused on it, watching as it danced on his skin. When he was within touching distance, he grazed his fingers along the bottom edge. He poked a finger out and waited. When it didn't burn, he pushed a hand. He waited for the flames that didn't come.

Lucius tilted his face down and closed his eyes as he pushed the back of his head out of the water. He inched higher until finally he turned his face upward. The air was warm compared to the ocean.

Lucius held his breath and slowly opened his eyes. He blinked a couple of times as his vision adjusted. His eyes stung, but they did not burn in his head. He felt Brutus and Demon below him, felt a hand brush his tail.

'*My king?*' Demon asked.

'*Should we pull him down?*' Brutus asked.

'*I'm well,*' Lucius managed to tell them.

He wanted to thank them for their friendship, for being there with him. He wanted to say so many things but knew those words were not necessary.

A boat caught his attention. The faint sound of strange music came from it as it neared. He opened his mouth, letting the air touch his tongue without breathing in. His mouth tingled, prickling like tiny needles being jabbed into his gums. Still, he did not burn.

Movement by the boat drew his notice, and he saw a flailing red missile fall from the deck. He focused his vision as it hit the water, sending a vibration over his sensitive skin. A woman?

The king gasped, realizing a woman had fallen into the water. The air filled his lungs at the involuntary reflex. He dove under, blowing bubbles from his mouth as he swam to save her. The twins came up behind him.

'*What is it?*' Brutus called.

'*Are you injured?*' Demon asked. '*Does it burn?*'

'*I saw something.*' The king darted through the water toward the ship. He dove deeper when he didn't see anyone kicking at the surface. '*In the water.*'

Just then, a large block passed by him, seemingly coming out of nowhere as it traveled to the bottom of the abyss. The glint of a shiny cord caught his attention, and then a leg. Out of instinct, he reached out, catching the human body before it sank past him. The heavy weight dragged him down with the person, and he was forced to thrust his tail to counter the pull.

The smell of blood in the water was unmistakable. It mingled with the seaweed-like drift of the mortal's long blonde hair.

It *was* a woman.

The king glanced up as the boat sailed away and then to her lifeless face. Instinct caused him to open his mouth wide and place his lips on hers. He inhaled sharply. Pulling the water from her lungs, he suctioned his mouth over hers. Her soft body was so delicate in his arms that he was sure she didn't stand a chance at survival. That didn't mean he stopped trying though.

As he tried to breathe for her, he let the heavy block pull them both down. Strands of her hair were in his mouth, but he didn't dare break the seal. The pressure of the abyss and their rapid descent might otherwise kill her.

Already she was as cold as the water. The dying heat from her body couldn't sustain her, so he wrapped his arms around her tightly and held her as close as he could. The anchor pulled them down, alleviating his need to swim as he instead did his best to guide the descent. She didn't fight his embrace. His sensitive skin detected her heartbeat and he tracked each thud with worry, fearful it might be her last.

How did the hunters do this? Time and time again, pulling ill-fated humans from the water, only to have them die on the way down? And still they went back and tried. That was true honor. There could be no doubting the hunters' nobility.

The law was clear. He knew because he'd declared it, but he'd never been made to follow this particular one. Since women were rare in Atlantes, and he had a dome full of lonely Merr, the king had decided it was best to try to satisfy the needs of both lonely Merr and dying humans. If a human was condemned to a watery death and could be saved, they were to try, even though the odds were not in their favor. Sometimes that meant pushing them to the surface so they could cling to a raft and be discovered by nearby ships. When there was no hope, it meant trying to bring them down.

Human life was so fragile, so delicate, like the woman in his arms. It was a wonder they'd managed to save any, and it was why they only attempted it with those destined to perish at sea.

'Where did she come from?' Brutus asked. 'There was no wreck.'

'The weight,' Lucius ordered in desperation, as he tried to keep his mouth over hers in the breathing kiss. It was the only chance she had to survive the dive toward the sea floor and to Atlantes.

The light from above dissipated into darkness. His Merr vision cut through the black with ease, and his eyes radiated a soft glow that reflected off the woman's face. Beyond them, he felt the creatures of the deep moving in the water. It was more an impression of vibrations and changes in the currents. If the Merr left the sea creatures alone, they normally avoided the Merr in return.

He listened to rather than saw Brutus and

Demon. They darted past him. The pull of her anchor lifted as the two hunters found the cord.

'*We can cut the rope with our fins,*' Demon said.

The cord jerked a few times and he knew they sawed at it with the sharp fins protruding from their forearms like defensive weapons. Suddenly, their descent slowed and he was able to control their path. He turned, angling them toward Atlantes and away from what appeared to be a squid of enormous proportions. The deeper they swam, the fiercer the creatures would become. In the deep, they did not resemble their surface-dwelling counterparts.

Lucius felt the faint beat of her heart as he pulled her as close as he could. He tried to breathe deep and fast, unsure how much air was the correct amount. It had been so long since he'd held a woman that the brush of her legs along his tail was torture. His lips tingled, but he didn't dare move them. If the seal broke, the pressure from being this deep would kill her faster than the water in her lungs. What choice did he have but to take her below? She was already almost dead, and whoever had tossed her into the ocean would not welcome her safe return to the surface.

'*Steady your breathing,*' Brutus instructed. '*You'll need your energy.*'

'*Well done, my king,*' Demon said with pride. '*Today you are one of us. You are a hunter!*'

Lucius was worried the man boasted too soon. They still had a long way to go until they made it home. She trembled violently in his arms, and he knew she didn't have long to live.

3

Damn it was cold.

Olivette's first instinct was to grab for blankets. Her hand met with something smooth. Her hair pulled down around her shoulders. Seeing the image of Tanner flash across her mind, she jerked violently and began to struggle. Arms held her tight and a gag pressed over her mouth.

When she opened her eyes, two blue dots of light looked at her from the darkness.

Unfortunately, her struggle wasn't very effective. Her numb limbs had lost feeling from the cold and she flopped around more than struck at her captor. As she became more aware, she realized the pull on her hair was the rush of water, as if her spirit glided through the ocean. The salt stung her eyes, and she had to close them.

Her temple throbbed where she'd hit her head when she had tried to escape after Tanner cornered her on the boat. No one had answered her cries for help. The music had been too loud. Now there was no music, only silence broken by the slow *thud, thud, thud* of her heart.

They rolled through the ocean, twisting and turning like a roller coaster. She's always hated amusement park rides, the jerking back and forth and the sickening feel of free falling. The motion sickness patch she'd had on during the boat trip had most likely come off, because she felt nauseous.

She tried to take a deep breath and realized the mouth around hers was giving her air. The man was breathing for her. That made no sense. She was lucid enough to know she was hallucinating.

Still, the man represented life, and she pressed her mouth more fully to his, gasping in what warm air she could deep into her burning lungs. The harder she panted, the worse she felt. They spun erratically as if a sudden current swept them out of control. An object knocked against her back and bounced off again. She gave a small scream of surprise. There was nothing she could do, nowhere to go, so she closed her eyes tight and prayed that the trip would soon be over.

She had no reasonable idea of how long they swam like that, or if she was even fully conscious for all of it, before light peeked through her closed lids. The stark contrast to the darkness forced her to fight the saltwater sting to look. A man's face emerged from the shadows, forming around the blue eyes. She caught a glimpse of another swimmer, half man, half fish, but the image was so brief she couldn't be sure what she saw was real.

For, if she wasn't still hallucinating, she'd been taken hostage by mermen.

The light seemed to be coming from an underwater facility. It grew brighter as they approached. They dove lower, along rocky inlets, until finally dipping into a tunnel. As frightened as she was, the idea of an entrance gave her hope that this ordeal might soon be over.

They emerged inside the light. The man drew her upward until they broke the surface. He unlatched his lips. Her head rolled back on her shoulders and she struggled to lift it. The impression of crystals on cave walls filtered past her vision. The air was sweet, but she didn't care as her lungs filled deeply again and again. She coughed, the briny taste in her mouth becoming pronounced now that she was breathing on her own. Her vision faded and she fought to stay awake.

Olivette was useless as they lifted her out of the water. Her ridiculous costume dripped water over the stone as two men lifted her up and set her against the cave wall. The one who had been carrying her leapt out of the water. He flipped a blue tail. The caudal fin clung to the rocks like wet silk.

She couldn't turn away, even when she perceived the two other men to be standing in the cave damp and naked. The blue merman shook his hands to dry them before gliding his fingers over his tail to flick water from it. The caudal fin stiffened, bloating as it morphed into feet. His tail tore apart, blue scales fading into tanned flesh. The fins on his forearms retracted as if stored in his muscles. When he stood, he too was naked. There was a blur of a strong chest, the flexing of an arm, a fisted hand. She waited for the glow to leave his eyes, but they remained an unnaturally bright blue, more brilliant than the gemstones reflecting light on the walls.

This cave wasn't big enough for all of them. Olivette felt the walls crowding in. Her breath rasped and she had to fight for each slow intake of air. A cool tear slid down an even colder cheek, or perhaps it was her dripping hair. She couldn't stop shivering, and she'd lost feeling in her limbs.

"Co-cold," she tried to whisper but the word was slurred.

The merman captor reached down and lifted her up. He held her against him like a limp rag doll, her toes skimming the ground. She didn't protest as the warmth of his body seeped into her. It wasn't enough.

"My king," one of the others said, "we should take her to Althea."

The merman lifted her into his arms. "Run ahead. Tell her we come."

He carried her through the caves. Olivette used all her energy to keep her eyes open, even when they couldn't fully focus. They passed from the primitive cave into an elegant hallway. Impressions of statutes in ancient garb swept past her. She thought to see one of the statues move. Footsteps sounded like bare feet on marble, the slap of skin and rock in a steady rhythm.

"My king...my king..." People spoke as if from far away.

The numbness spread. She could no longer feel her shoulder or hips. The only sensation she had was the painful draw of her chest and the bounce of her neck as the man carried her. Her head shifted, turning from the man to the passing walls. Blue, yellow, and white tiles created a mesmerizing pattern. They flashed as light reflected off their glossy veneer. She stared until the repetitious pattern became hypnotic, lulling her sluggish mind with the promise of rest. They passed under an archway and the break in the pattern shocked her back from the brink.

"Althea isn't in the palace," a voice said.

"Where is she?" the man holding her demanded. "This one's heart feels weak. We need the healer."

"With Aidan in the village. Demon went to search for her." A hand touched her head and angled it so she again stared at his chest. "You must make her warm and dry."

"Send the healer to my home when you find her." The man holding her began to run, jostling Olivette. The numbness and pain were too much. Let the darkness take her. She no longer cared. Anything to make this strange journey come to an end.

4

Lucius set the unconscious woman in his bed and inelegantly jerked the wet clothing from her body. The red and white dress sloshed as he dropped it on the floor. The leg coverings looked like a fisherman's net. They weren't as wet, but he tore them off as well. He forgot what the new arrivals called the undergarment over the breasts, but he pulled at the back of hers until it broke free.

When she was out of the wet clothes, he arranged her limbs into a more comfortable position on his bed and drew his blankets over her. As much as he wanted to look at her naked form, he didn't allow himself the luxury. He watched to see if the warmth of the dry covers would help revive her. It didn't appear to.

He left the bedroom and hurried out to the hallway to see if Althea was coming. The palace hall was empty. He glanced around his home, trying to find something to help him know what to do. Though larger in size than most, in many ways his home was just like the others at the palace. The square living area was the center of the home, leading to an office, sleeping chambers, and a bathing room. He ran to his office. He'd spent many nights alone at his desk in isolation. There was nothing of use unless he dumped parchment scrolls over her.

He rushed to a small table. What was he doing? He took his meals in the dining hall, so there was no need for a place to dine.

Flustered, he turned in circles. All the decor had been tributes given to him by his subjects, including the furniture. His people had nothing if not time to perfect their trades. The couches were low with no backs and covered wool cushions. The chairs were hand carved. Vases were intricately engraved and painted. Tapestries depicted great scenes from their proudest moments in history.

He grabbed a blanket from the couch and hurried back to the bedroom to toss it on top of her before searching for more.

Lucius again found himself looking down the

palace hall, anxiously awaiting help that did not come. He wished the healer was there to tell him what to do. It was bad enough that coming out of the ocean left his kind filled with the need for sexual release. Passions ran deep in the Merr, and it was pure torture. They called it the affliction, and if they didn't manage it they started to feel ill and their thoughts would become unfocused. His blood felt thick with desire, and it clouded his judgment. He didn't like the fact that his biological needs were trying to take over his thoughts. Just another cruel jest of the gods—deep sexual desires with little opportunity to fulfill them with a woman.

Unmated Merr, both men and women, were given pleasure instruments to deal with their afflictions. Taking a lover from amongst the population was discouraged. For a time, he'd had a lover—Maia. He supposed it had been good between them. It must have been. However, she'd wanted to be queen and he'd not wanted to marry. In truth, he hadn't wanted to give her that much power. Her temperament wasn't suited to leadership. So, she declared herself ruler of the Olympians and he'd lost his lover. She became his enemy and now they were at war. Eternity was a long time to hold a grudge over old relationships.

He went back to the bedroom to check on his ward. She was still shivering and her pale color had moved into the blue spectrum. None of that appeared favorable.

His naked body was dirty, covered with saltwater residue, and he hesitated before moving to touch her. He laid next to her, cradling her in the blanket so their skin didn't touch. He rocked and held her, willing her to take his warmth. She shivered violently and when it didn't stop, he scooped her up and carried her wrapped in the bedding toward the shower.

With a pull of a cord, warm water rained down onto a platform. Merr did not transform in fresh water. He sat with her on the platform, cradling her to his chest as he leaned over to block the rain from her face. Water soaked the blankets, and he hoped the heat would be enough.

Lucius didn't know what else to do. It was still surreal that he'd saved a human woman. Was this a sign from the gods? The first time he'd felt the surface air in thousands of years, and a woman was dropped down into the water for him to capture. It forced him to bring her back down, to leave the surface. Were they not happy that he'd dared to break free of the underwater prison? Or was it a reward for bravery?

The memory of the surface air in his lungs, sharply tingling, scared him now that he had a moment to think about what he'd done, how close he'd come to death. In many ways, he hadn't expected Lady Bridget's theories about the seaweed to work. He was ashamed to admit that a part of him had hoped to die on the surface, for the loneliness and the years to be over. Instead, he rescued his first human.

The messages from the gods made no sense.

Maybe they were not messages at all. Maybe there were no signs, only the tediousness of existence.

Poseidon had cursed them down and forgotten about them. They were disowned children. An embarrassment. Discarded. Buried at sea.

"Not much matters anymore," Lucius whispered to the unconscious woman, not knowing what he should say to her. "My life is endless. The gods wouldn't even let the air stop me, but you're fragile, aren't you? I could let you go and save you from all of this. I know the law. I made the law. I know I'm supposed to try, but I'll tell you a secret. I don't always know what is best. I just decide which laws and they all follow me without question even though it was my boasting pride that struck us down. Do you want immortality?" He held her tighter in the soaked bedding. "It is in Poseidon's webbed hands if you live, but I would appreciate it if you tried. You made the dive down. That's a good start. Now I need you to open your eyes. I wish Althea the Healer was here to do this. She would be much better at it than I am."

The woman didn't move.

"By order of the king," he said in his most commanding tone. "Wake up."

Nothing.

'*Can you hear me?*' he tried telepathically.

Still nothing.

"Please don't die?" he questioned in a gentler voice.

That too did not appear to work.

"You are strange creatures, you women from the surface world. Definitely not like I remember you." Lucius rocked her slowly. "I am sorry I ruined your dress. I think I tore it, but I promise if you wake up, I'll have the seamstress replace it with ten new ones. I am told women like new garments."

With that, he thought to see her eyelashes flutter. A sign? It had to be.

"Make that twenty new garments," he said with a

nod, feeling as if he'd made some progress. "You're the ward of the king after all, so it only seems fitting."

She stopped shivering, and he studied her wet face. When he'd breathed for her, it had not been the kiss of lovemaking, but in many ways, it was more intimate. He'd transferred life into her, breathing for them both as they dove. He'd felt the moment she awoke, saw the flash of her eyes before she closed them tight. She'd tried to draw the air from him faster than he could give it, and his lungs had burned in pain at the attempt.

He continued to rock her in his lap as he searched beneath the wet blankets to feel her temperature. The chill was gone. He held his hand flat against her back, willing her to take whatever energy she needed from him.

"Thank you," he thought he heard her say, but the word was so faint and the sound of falling water too loud. He could have easily imagined it.

He held her tighter to his chest, stroking his fingers along her wet back. "Don't die."

"My king," Althea called, drawing his attention toward the shower room door.

The slender woman appeared in the doorway and took stock of the room. She was well dressed in the ancient fashion—draped in fine linen rubbed with oil to make the material shine. The dark patterns along the hems were made to represent flowing seaweed. Two metal discs held the garments at her shoulders. The engravings were worn from centuries of polishing. She wore her brown hair in an intricate coil around the crown of her head. Tiny metal beads were stuck in the braid to create the illusion of a crown though she was not royal.

The healer crossed to the shower cord and pulled it to make the water stop. "Why do you have her in the water? Mortals need to be dry. Bring her to the bed."

"She was cold," he explained, pushing to his feet while still holding her in his arms. Water dripped around them, most heavily coming from the wet blankets. "And the heat from the water worked to warm her."

"And all this moisture in the air will fill her chest and settle there. She'll die of a lung illness before she even regains consciousness." Althea held up her hand. "Leave the wet blankets. You're making a mess."

Lucius didn't care about a mess, but he maneuvered the woman in his arms and let the water-soaked covers drop to the floor with a heavy splat. Following Althea's instructions left him carrying a naked woman against his already afflicted body, and he found walking uncomfortable. He placed her damp body on his bed and stepped back while the healer drew an extra blanket around her.

"Leave us," Althea ordered. "If I have learned anything from watching you men bring down women, it's that you only get in the way."

"Will she live?" Lucius asked.

"If the gods will it," Althea answered. She lifted her hands to hover along the woman's chest, sensing for illness. "The best thing you can do for any of us is to go back in that shower and take care of your affliction and let me take care of my patient."

Lucius glanced down to where his arousal stood tall and painful. Curse the gods for this inconvenience. He eyed the wet red clothes he'd thrown on the floor. Water seeped from the material to form a puddle. He didn't want to leave. What if this was the last moments of her life?

The gods had distracted his surfacing with a woman. Was she an offering to make him content beneath the waves? To stop him from returning to the surface? Did the gods see them rising to the top and want them kept in their place? Would the decisions he made affect the outcome of this woman's story?

"I can hear you breathing," the healer muttered. She'd closed her eyes as she touched the woman's chest.

Lucius walked back, watching what was happening in his room as long as he could before the image disappeared from view. Hurrying to the shower to bathe properly, he couldn't get the image of the red-soaked garment on his bedroom floor out of his mind. Perhaps it was what it represented—the red blood of mortality soaked by the ocean, another relic from the surface world—or perhaps it was simply that the material had touched and held soft breasts and feminine curves in a way he could not.

Lucius found his soapy hand on his member as he stroked himself under the rain of the shower. She had to live. He was king, and he would command her to do so. He imagined her breath was still in his lungs from when he breathed for her on the dive down. The soft skin of her body beneath the wet blankets had been so delicate to the touch, very unlike the pleasure nymph dolls they were given to fight the affliction.

She had to live. She had to live.

Lucius groaned as he met his release. The bitter-sweet sensation eased the physical ache inside his body but did nothing for his lonely soul.

5

"SOME THINK this afterlife is a horrible place, but I don't think it's all that bad."

Aidan wouldn't stop talking even though she didn't open her eyes again. Olivette had made that mistake once already, and her babysitter had since felt the need to fill the silence. First, it had been a woman who wouldn't quit touching her, and now it was this man who wouldn't stop talking at her.

"Mortality is so final. Think of all the things we can do and learn if we are not on a finite time schedule. Anyway, where was I? So they stopped worshipping Poseidon and began to worship themselves as gods upon the earth, taking what they were given for granted and becoming lazy. They raided their neighbors, took more than they could use in five lifetimes... well, mortal lifetimes."

"You said this part already," Olivette muttered, still not opening her eyes.

"I knew you were awake, my lady, but I wanted to make sure the information was heard. It's important we do this before you come out of your euphoria. Otherwise, it's a lot harder to process that you're living in the lost city of Atlantes with merfolk."

Olivette finally looked at him. Aidan wore a kind expression that shone from his brown eyes. Compared to the giant merman who'd carried her through the water, this man was slighter in stature, with short brown hair. His brown wool shirt and pants seemed straight out of a hippy commune. "I would hardly use the word euphoric for what I'm feeling right now. I feel like there is a fifty-pound weight on my chest. My throat is raw. I'm having nightmares about tentacles. And you're a mermaid."

"Man," Aidan corrected. "I'm a merman. I assure you, I am no maid."

"My head is throbbing." She pulled the covers over her head, not wanting to argue the English language. She frowned and pulled them back off. "If you're Greek, and the gods cast you down, how are you speaking English?"

"Don't try to find the rational in the irrational," he instructed. "It's part of the magic of the place."

"I don't believe in magic," she said, partly to be difficult.

"But here you are, talking to a converted merman at the bottom of the deep ocean," Aidan laughed.

She glanced around the lavish bedroom. A circular pedestal held the rectangular bed like an indoor gazebo, with a column at each corner. The blue, yellow, and white décor reminded her of being carried through the palace, blurred memories of tiled walls and ancient statues. Each large decorative vase on the floor stood well over six feet tall. She could imagine the hundreds of thousands of dollars each one would go for on the open market. The creamy-yellow blanket over her body was thin, but she found the room neither too hot nor too cold.

"Converted? You mean you chose this?"

"Like you, it chose me. I was rescued from a ship-wreck. I was born in eighteen-ninety-three in a southern county of Scotland." As he said the words, she started to detect a hint of a Scottish accent, as if what she expected to hear was what she *could* actually hear. He continued, "I worked as an historical scholar. We were sailing on the *Bella Donna* to Africa to explore the great pyramids. Everyone was very excited about the buried treasures of the desert. Our boat was attacked by a scylla—do you know about the scylla?"

Olivette shook her head in denial.

"It's a sad thing. When the Merr are out in the isolation of the ocean for too long, they go insane. Eventually, that insanity causes them to lose themselves. They begin to take on the traits of the water, losing their identity, their pigmentation, their reasoning, becoming angry water spirits. In their confusion, they attack any signs of life from the surface world. That's what happened to our ship. A scylla attacked it and we sank. I was fortunate that the Merr hunters were tracking the scylla to bring it home. The captain of the *Bella Donna* was superstitious and believed women on a ship to be unlucky, so it was only us men. For me, that proved right."

"But your ship crashed and there were no women. How is that lucky?"

"Since there were no women onboard Demon the Hunter saved me and brought me here."

He was saved by a demon? Why not? It's not like this situation could get any stranger. "You're saying if there was a woman they would have saved her instead of you and you would have drowned?"

"Exactly." Aiden nodded. "It is good to see you talking. Do you have a name?"

"Yes," she managed with a small cough.

"And it is?"

"Olivette Waller."

"It is a pleasure to make your acquaintance, Lady Olivette," Aidan said with a gentlemanly nod.

"What do they want with us?"

"To save us. To learn from us. To show the gods they have changed and are good people." Aidan waved a dismissive hand as if she asked all the wrong questions.

"What if I don't want to convert? What if I want them to bring me home?" she asked.

"It doesn't work that way," he said. "Those who come down cannot go back up."

"So they'll hold me prisoner because I can't swim that far?" Olivette tried to sit up, but her desire to do so was no match for her physical inability to move.

"Because you're one of us, or you will be soon." Aidan sat back in his chair and contemplated her. "What job did you have above?"

"It doesn't matter," she whispered. She didn't meet his gaze as she turned her attention to the wall and tears seeped out of her eyes. She wasn't sad, necessarily, but weak and overwhelmed and tired. She was becoming a mermaid?

"Lady Bridget was one of the first to come down in recent times. She was working as a scientist aboard her vessel when it was wrecked by the scylla, and has contributed greatly to the community with her knowledge and research. Lady Lyra has provided many fashionable designs to the seamstress. Lady Victoria discovered a way to cure the scylla when we bring them back from the ocean. She nearly died when she became one herself. Before that, every creature died a horrible death. Now there is hope that we can bring our people home. And Lady Cass—"

"I'm a florist," Olivette interrupted so that he'd stop listing out every accomplished woman in Atlantes. He was beginning to sound like her mother, pointing out how she could be living her life better. "I arrange flowers into pretty configurations. But since that business failed, I have also walked dogs, waited tables, delivered cars from one lot to another, worked concessions at a race track, cleaned houses, cleaned offices, cleaned pools, and had the misfortune of signing on to serve cocktails aboard an evening party cruise dressed like Mrs. Claus' slutty sister, even though it's spring. So, unless there is a big call for fish walkers or elf waitresses, I'm not sure I'm going to have all that much to contribute to your society."

Her throat hurt, but the diatribe had been worth it. She felt a little better after the rant.

"You were serving drinks when the scylla hit your boat?" Aidan verified. "Is it true the king brought you back? Not one of the hunters, Demon or Brutus?"

"King?"

"King Lucius," Aidan clarified.

"I don't know who he was." Olivette remembered a man holding her, swimming with her, carrying her into the rain and then into softness. But the images were a blur. She saw a flash of bright blue eyes, of longer dark brown hair, of a blue tail coming out of the ocean onto a rocky ledge, only to mold into strong human legs.

"But you remember your ship being wrecked?"

"I remember..." She took a deep breath as she recalled being assaulted by Tanner. She felt the memory of his hands trying to grip their way up her skirt and pressed her legs together. Another hot tear slid down the side of her cheek. "Who is King Lucius?"

"Quite right, I should finish telling you the story.

King Lucius has ruled the Merr since before they became Merr. He is the reason Poseidon cursed these people. I have been collecting the stories of those who were there when it happened. Not many like to talk about it, but I have been able to piece together this much. The short version is that Lucius proclaimed he would never die, for he never wished to leave his bountiful kingdom paradise on Earth. That the land he'd created with his sword and his will was more beautiful than any kingdom of the gods, and they could stand to learn a few things from the Atlantean people."

"And Poseidon didn't like that, broke off a piece of land, and buried them under the ocean," Olivette concluded succinctly. "I'm sure the god said something clever like, 'If you want this land and immortality so badly, well fine, take that'."

"Someone has told you this?" Aidan asked, appearing hurt that his tale was taken away from him.

"No, it's just easy to deduce where the tale was going. Man pisses off gods. Gods put man in his place. We're under the water in what looks like a giant dome—if my fuzzy memory of the dive serves—so I can only guess how they were punished." She sighed. Her voice was becoming fainter. "Are you sure you're not a fiction writer? It's an interesting bedtime story, and I can't come up with a better explanation right now."

"It's not fiction. It's the truth. Poseidon cast Ataran down, trapping them so they could never walk on mortal soil again. They can't even breathe the air. Atlantes is doomed to drift along the bottom of the ocean at the whim of the currents." Aidan's tone wasn't as conversational as before. "King Lucius was a man of his time, so you must not think poorly of him. He is a very good king, and he saved your life."

"You don't know what happened. The boat I was on didn't get hit by anything. It didn't sink."

"I know that if the king saved you, then you didn't have any other options and would have died," Aidan argued.

"You said Ataran. I thought we were in Atlantes."

"We are. Ataran is what the country is called, the actual land. Atlas is the city. Atlantes is the whole thing," he explained.

"Ataran. Atlantes. Atlas. Aidan." The headache became worse and she didn't want to talk anymore.

"The Merr do like the beginning of the alphabet, don't they?"

"Why, yes, they—" Aidan began to laugh.

"What are you doing? I said to watch her, not tire her out." The healer appeared in the doorway. "Aidan, I told you, she doesn't need to hear your stories right now. She needs sleep."

"Althea," Olivette muttered. Another 'A'.

"Yes, my lady?" the healer queried.

Olivette didn't answer as she closed her eyes. All she wanted was silence and to be left alone.

"Aidan, leave," Althea ordered.

"King Lucius," Aidan's voice stuttered. "How long have you been—?"

"Aidan," the healer insisted.

Olivette turned her attention toward the door. Through the doorframe, she saw someone push up from a sitting position on the floor. She hadn't noticed his arrival.

"Aye, yes, yes, I'm leaving. I'll see you at home, my beautiful," Aidan told Althea as he left.

Althea placed her hands on Olivette's face. Olivette tried to jerk away from the overly familiar touch. The healer's hands radiated heat, sending tiny vibrations through her skull. The pain in her head began to lessen. Hands moved to hold her throat, and

Olivette coughed as the fingers tightened. She breathed easier.

Olivette watched, no longer trying to stop the healer. The touch continued over her body, moving almost mechanically along her chest and stomach. Her flesh tingled. She met the blue eyes of her merman rescuer. The king of the Merr. King Lucius.

The king didn't speak, didn't smile or frown. He watched as one would an unamusing show. His clothing appeared straight out of Ancient Greece. The white, rectangular shirt draped over his solid chest. Two brooches held the sleeves together at his shoulders. A gold belt wrapped his waist. The shirt fell to his thighs. Beneath he wore snuggly fitted pants. A purple sash draped one shoulder before reaching around his waist and was held in place by one of the brooches. The leather sandals appeared out of place with such stately attire.

Suddenly, Althea leaned down and pressed her lips to Olivette's, breathing into her mouth.

Olivette gasped in shock at the unexpected contact. The woman's breath filled her lungs with the same healing energy.

When the healer pulled away, she withdrew her hands and stood. She wobbled lightly on her feet. "I have done all I can, my king. She should rest as long as she needs to. I must do the same."

Olivette touched her throat. The soreness was gone.

"Thank you, Althea," the king answered. He nodded at her as she slowly walked from the room.

6

"How do you feel?" Lucius found it difficult to meet his ward's eye. He'd heard nearly everything Aidan had said to her. Perhaps it was for the best she knew his sins. If not Aidan, someone would have told her the story of their curse eventually.

"Better," Olivette answered. "I don't know what the healer did, but..."

"Healing has always been Lady Althea's gift, an invaluable one of recent years." He thought of the other women his people had managed to save from the surface world.

She studied him for a very long time, so long that he shifted his weight, anxious for her to speak. In some ways, it had been easier when she was unconscious. He didn't have to think about the words that would come out of his mouth. Normally, conversing with someone wasn't his weakness. As a king, he had to be adept at putting people at ease with a playful charm. Some were intimidated by his power. Others were angry about a decision he had made. All his subjects were like his children, and he the supreme father meant to protect and guide them. It was a heavy burden.

He glanced at the floor, wondering if he should leave the woman to rest as Althea suggested. Before he could go, she finally spoke.

"I thought all kings wore crowns."

"Not in my home." Lucius gave a meaningful glance around the elegant bedroom, prompting her to do the same.

"I knew this looked a little too stylish to be a hospital." Olivette gave a small laugh and pushed herself up to sit on the bed. He saw her struggle and instantly stepped up onto the circular platform to assist. He slid a hand behind her back and helped her up. Althea had dressed his ward in a plain cotton gown to keep her comfortable while she slept, but that didn't mean his mind couldn't picture every detail beneath the material. "I'd curtsy, but I have a feeling I'd collapse on the floor if I tried."

"You must rest." Lucius pulled away from her.

Touching her reminded him of his earlier shower. Fine, his earlier *eight* showers. For some reason, his affliction had run deep after this last swim in the ocean. "Though, I take it as a positive sign that you have awakened after three days."

"Three days?" She appeared surprised. He nodded. "I didn't realize it had been so long. It felt like seconds. Well, the part in the ocean felt like years, but sleeping felt like seconds."

"It is natural that you would need to recover." He made a move for the door. "I have food for you when you are ready to dine. Let me know and I will bring it in to you."

"I'm not sure I want to be here," Olivette announced to stop him from leaving.

Lucius glanced around his bedroom. He's always thought of it as a fine room. "Is this not to your liking? It is the only bedroom in my section of the palace, but I will find you another. I will see which of the hunters is not yet back at the palace and—"

"In Atlantes," she clarified. "I'm not sure I want to be down here, in Atlantes. I'll make a horrible mermaid. I was never a strong swimmer. Aidan pointed out that I have nothing to contribute to this society. Please, can I go home?"

Guilt hit him at her words. Had he made the

wrong decision in rescuing her? Was it a selfish deci-sion? He hadn't considered his actions too intently at the time. He'd simply acted on instinct, seeing her fall into the water as a sign.

"For now, this is your home," he said. "You should focus on your recovery."

"Don't placate me." She pushed her legs off the side of the bed. "Tell it to me straight. You're not letting me leave, are you?"

"I can't. Once someone comes to Atlantes, their fate is sealed." He watched for signs of hysteria. She remained calm on the exterior though he could detect the subtle shifting of her eyes as she consid-ered his words.

"You can't swim me up like you brought me down?"

"No," he stated.

"What if I were to go to the ocean myself?"

"You'd drown."

"So, stay or die?"

"No, not die. Drown. It is the final process in your transformation to become a mermaid. You won't survive the swim up until after you transform. The change in pressure would kill you in your current state. It's a miracle you survived the dive down. And, once you change, you won't be able to return to the surface because..."

He hesitated, remembering the feel of surface air in his lungs. They had decided not to tell the public he'd survived the test, but he didn't want to lie to his ward either. If his people found out before he was ready to enact laws pertaining to surfacing, chaos would erupt in their paradise. He didn't need more chaos, not with the ongoing problems with the Olympians.

"Because?" she prompted.

"Because the Merr do not touch surface air." It wasn't a lie. As a rule, they didn't.

Her eyes narrowed. "But someone did, didn't they? I thought I saw a hand poke out of the water, but convinced myself it was a dolphin. It wasn't, was it? It was one of you."

He gasped. "You saw me?"

"That was you?"

He took a step into the room, looming over her. "You can't tell anyone what you witnessed."

She leaned away from him. "What did I witness?"

"The others can't know that I surfaced. My people have not breathed or touched surface air since we came down. It should kill us, but we've been working on a cure. It's too soon to create hope where there might only be disappointment. My people have accepted their fates because they assume that this is all there can ever be."

"How do you cure air that's poisonous to you?"

"We discovered that a small sect of mermaids called the Olympians were eating a special seaweed diet. There were rumors they were breaking the surface and luring humans to their deaths, taking some of them as slaves. We have no proof of this but have been analyzing their diet. The day I rescued you from drowning, I was the first to surface to test out the theory."

Olivette studied him with a strange expression on her face. "Okay."

"What?"

"Nothing. I said okay," she dismissed.

"What are you thinking? I see," he gestured toward her face, "something here."

"I find your story a little peculiar."

"How so?"

"Why would a king be the first to test out a theory that would most likely lead to his death?" she questioned. "It seems odd to me, especially when I gather from Aidan that you don't have an election system in place and you've been king since the dawn of time."

"It is my duty to protect my people."

"If you say so, but it sounds a little bit like you're either, one, an adrenaline junkie who likes the rush of doing stupid things, or two, don't care if you die." She eyed him. "You don't look stupid to me."

The succinctness of her deduction caused a sharp pain to radiate through his chest. If this woman, who had been in Atlantes for less than a week, saw his secret, who else detected it?

He crossed his arms protectively over his chest as he stood in the doorway.

Her eyes widened slightly as if she were reconsidering her words. "But what do I know. I just arrived and am probably still delirious from the dive."

"No, you're not delirious," he stated.

"Do you want to talk about it?" She moved over on the bed and patted it. "I worked in a bar for three months. I'm told I'm a great listener."

Lucius approached her cautiously at the invitation. He couldn't remember the last time someone offered to listen to his problems. Normally, they *brought* him problems. The invitation did not feel sexual, but that didn't stop yet another wave of affliction from attacking his body. His arms ached to hold her, to lie on the bed and cradle her to his chest, to whisper into her ear, to kiss her neck...

"You don't have to talk about it, just sit with me," she offered.

Lucius sat on the edge of the bed, his back stiff as he refused to sink too comfortably into it. He glanced at her.

"Is anyone else here? Can they hear us?" Olivette leaned to look out the door.

"No. They will knock before they enter my home."

"Why did you try to hurt yourself?" Her voice remained soft and gentle, like the undulating currents of a calm ocean.

Lucius started to answer but stopped himself. He was king. He was not allowed to be weak. "What happened to you? Why were you thrown into the ocean like that? Why did those loud humans not try to save you?"

She glanced up at the ceiling as if contemplating the surface far, far above. "Since my business went under, it's been a little tough trying to find steady work, so I was waitressing on that boat. Things got a little rough with one of the partygoers and I ended up in the ocean."

Lucius began to nod his head, turning to look at

the floor, before the full scope of what she might be saying hit him. He stood and again stepped off the platform, this time in agitation. "Are you saying you were...?" He glanced down her body before turning his attention toward the ocean's surface. His breathing became choppy with anger. The urge to swim up and find that boat was strong. He fisted his hands. He should have overturned it when he had the chance.

"He tried. I screamed and managed to hit him." Olivette touched the side of her head where he'd seen the wound as she drifted past him in the ocean. "We must have struggled because I hit my head and became too dazed to fight back. No one came. The music was too loud. I remember being dragged to the side of the boat and then falling. The shock of the cold water woke me but by then it was too late. I was being pulled under. The salt stung my cheek and choked my lungs and..." A tear slid down her face. "I remember not wanting to die. I was so scared. And then there you were, holding me, breathing for me."

Lucius relaxed some to hear she had not been violated, but his anger still simmered for the man who had disrespected a woman in such a way.

"Thank you for saving me." The bed shifted, and she touched his shoulder. "When I ask to go back to the surface, I don't intend to sound ungrateful. I didn't want to die in the ocean."

"You can't go back," he said, not daring to move lest her hand leave him. All his attention focused on the tingling sensation her touch caused. "If this makes you unhappy, then I am to blame for that as well."

"Why did you go to the surface? Surely someone else would have attempted to test your air theory." Her fingers made small linear movements against him.

The tingling became more intense, traveling down his back to focus on his stomach. The affliction grew, and he adjusted his hips without trying to draw attention to it. "It was my duty to go. It is my fault we're down here. How can I ask anyone else to take the risk?"

Her hand pulled away.

"I wanted to go."

He wasn't sure why he said the words out loud. Her hand returned, this time touching his back in longer caresses, urging him to speak.

"I have been king since what feels like the beginning of time. I have tried to name a successor so I may stop, but this life does not end and my people refuse to acknowledge another ruler. My being king gives them the normality they crave, a tie to the past. I am king because I have always been, and will always be."

"That is a lot of responsibility for one man. Do you not have someone to help carry the burden?" Her hand stopped. It was if he could read her thoughts with the movement of her fingers.

"No. I never married. When I took the crown, I didn't realize how long my reign would be, or how heavy the weight would become. When I was mortal, I thought I wanted eternity. I thought I wanted to be a god. I was a fool, and did not understand the breadth of what anything meant."

Her hand pressed fully against his shoulder. She hesitated before she took his hand. They sat on the bed. "Then you did go up to the surface to die, didn't you?"

"To die...to do something...to find an end to this cursed existence." He watched her fingers intertwine with his. "It could be any of those things. I don't know why for certain."

"What things *do* you know for certain? What things gave you a reason to carry on and live before this urge to surface found you?"

"Why do you care?"

She touched his face, turning his head so that his

gaze met hers. "You saved me. I feel it's my duty to return the favor."

"Hope. That is what I have held on to." Lucius studied her, unsure what to do with his hands. Did he return the gentle caress? Did he hold the one in his lap to continue to hide the effects of the affliction?

She leaned closer and her voice became softer. "Hope for what?"

"I hope as we all hope—that one day the curse will end and we'll again stand in the sunlight."

"What else?" Her voice was softer still.

"That the gods would choose me, bless me." His voice dropped to match hers in tone.

"Bless you how?"

"With a family, a wife," he paused and lowered his eyes, "with love."

"I imagine it is very lonely down here." Olivette's eyes lowered to his mouth. "Even more so for a king."

"Should I have pushed you back up to the surface and hoped they came back for you?" He liked the feeling of her being close, of her soft breath against his chin. The truth was, she made him nervous as if all decision-making logic swam right out of his head. He didn't know what to say or do. His hand began to lift toward her and he forced it back down to his lap.

"They would not have returned. Everyone was too drunk. They probably didn't realize I was missing until the next day when I didn't stop to pick up my paycheck. Even then, I doubt Patrick would have reported it to the police. He didn't come off as the most aboveboard employer. I don't believe my neighbors will think anything is wrong. We barely run into each other as it is. The work agency that contracts me by the job won't expect me in, especially if I don't answer their calls. I have friends, but we're all used to being busy; they might just think I'm working. My landlord will notice when I don't pay my rent in two weeks. He might say something when I don't turn up after another two. I don't talk to my mother as often as I should, so she won't think anything about it." She took a deep breath and placed her hand on his. Her fingers trembled. "I don't know what you remember of the surface world, but it can be very lonely up there, too."

"I..." Lucius tried to think of the perfect thing to say but again failed. What was it about this woman that made him doubt himself? "I will make sure you are welcome here."

"Thank you for not letting me die." She leaned closer and he could barely think.

"Thank you...for not being angry that...I saved

your life." The words kept coming out in a stuttering mess as if he'd not spent the past centuries being thoughtful and diplomatic.

She gave a small laugh. "Fair enough."

"I have feelings," he whispered, unable to stop himself from glancing down at her lips.

"I have feelings, too," she answered just as softly. Her lips curled into an amazing smile. "What are your feelings?"

He wanted to kiss her, but that hardly felt appropriate, given her newly arrived status, her illness, and the fact she was his ward and he was charged as the king to take care of her.

At that moment, he felt the loneliness worse than before. The ache inside him became so bitter and hard that he had to put space between them or he'd scream with the agony of it.

Lucius stood. "You need rest. I will leave you."

"I'm sorry. You said you had no queen. I didn't realize you were seeing someone else." There was questioning in her tone.

"I see many people." He frowned.

"'Seeing' as in 'dating'."

His frown deepened.

"That you have a lover already," she stated bluntly.

"Maia?" Lucius stiffened in shock that she would know about that. He did not hear Aidan talking about Maia. "No. We have not been lovers for many, many years. Things did not end well between us. Who told you of her?"

"You just did." She drew her feet back onto the bed. "You must have cared about her."

"I did care, but I did not love her, and that became a problem," he answered. "Some believed I should have married her and stopped her from defecting to Mt. Olympus to start her own mermaid cult. But I believe she would have been worse as my queen. I wish this war we are in could have been avoided, but the Olympians have gone too far. The hunters are in the forest looking for her now to bring her in."

Olivette stayed sitting on the bed as she stared at him.

"Naturally, I feel bad about this, but I cannot allow her to keep drowning humans and taking males as slaves. Plus, she started attacking the dome. If this dome collapsed, all the souls within would become lost."

"The scylla," she reasoned.

"Yes."

"And I thought politics on the surface world were

complicated." Olivette gave a small shake of her head. "Atlantes. Poseidon. Curses. Mermaid cults. Slaves. Scylla. Surface air and seaweed. Crazy ex-lovers. No wonder you're a little disheartened right now. You clearly must have a lot on your mind. Those are grave responsibilities you carry."

Lucius nodded. How was it she saw things so clearly? It was as if she looked inside him and read his soul, his mind, his troubles. Had the breathing kiss on the way down connected them somehow? Is that why the hunters had all ended up married to the women they saved? Did that mean this woman would become his...

Lucius couldn't finish the thought, couldn't allow his hope to take him there. "I should let your rest, as the healer instructed. Anything you require, simply ask and I will do my best."

7

OLIVETTE FELT the pull of the merman king. It was a cosmic force, calling her body closer to his. She ached to make contact. When she looked at him, a weakness filled her. At first she thought it was because she'd been sick, but this was unlike any illness she'd ever had. It manifested inside her head, a dull ache that radiated down her spine and grew worse the farther away he moved. The less they touched, the shakier she became.

When he tried to step out of the room, she felt as if her lungs were on fire, drowning yet again.

"Please, stay," she gasped, needing him to come back.

He arched a brow and reentered.

"So, no girlfriend?" She gave a small smile. "No lover?"

"Not at the present time," he answered.

The brightness of his eyes struck her yet again. They were the color of the Caribbean water. She imagined him to be the eye of the storm, and if he pulled away from her, that is when the turbulence started.

Olivette stood. "Then I don't understand."

"Understand?"

He appeared confused, but how could that be? She'd sent out all the signals. She'd touched his arm, leaned close, puckered her lips. She'd been unable to stop herself. She needed to be close to him.

Olivette reached for his hand and pulled it away from where he shielded his erection from her. The headache subsided as the heat radiated from his body. She closed her eyes and breathed deeply. She drew his hand so that it looped with hers behind her back as she stepped closer. Her lungs no longer burned and the trembling stopped, but she still felt weak.

"I don't understand how you can't feel this," she whispered, soaking in his nearness. "It started when we were in the ocean, and you breathed for me. You held my life inside you and kept me safe. I dreamed of the rain and you were there, shielding me from it, keeping me warm. And today, when you walked into the room, I felt better."

"Althea has many talents," he explained.

"No." She shook her head in denial, looking up at him. Her body pressed fully against his chest and she held his hand behind her back. "It wasn't Althea. She helped, but it was you."

"I...am..." He tried to speak, but it was as if the words were trapped in his throat.

Olivette felt his desire for her and it amplified her own. Her emotions surged, crushing any logic that might try to override what her body wanted. She lifted on her toes, wanting to breathe in his life force, wanting that adrenaline, the excitement and fear she'd felt on the dive down. She wanted to live. That was the force calling her to be next to him—life.

Her lips parted as she pressed her mouth to his. At first, it was not with the intent of seducing him into a kiss, but as flesh touched flesh, she moved her lips and breathed deeply.

He gasped, and she pulled back to study his face.

The harsh pants of air between them punctuated the silence. She leaned forward again, more insistently. Their lips moved awkwardly before finding a rhythm.

Olivette let go of the hand she held behind her back. He pressed into her, compelling her to move closer. She ran her fingers through his hair. Tiny shocks of electricity zapped wherever they touched. She moaned, needing more. Releasing her hold on him, she reached to pull her gown over her head and tossed it aside.

Lucius' eyes pierced hers with a predatory grace and he took a step forward, then another. She kept her gaze locked on his. Olivette let him walk her back to the bed. He pulled his shirt from his chest and threw it aside. It landed on one of the tall vases. Her heel hit the platform, and he reached for her naked waist to lift her onto it. As he stepped up to join her, his body pressed hard against hers.

This time when they kissed, their lips moved in perfect unison. Lucius pressed forward so that she lay on the bed. Everything about him seemed to consume her—his heat, his scent, the electric brush of his flesh. When he touched her, his hands sent a vibration over her that tickled her nerves to awareness.

She tugged the pants from his hips. The length of his arousal brushed her thigh. His hands seemed to explore everywhere at once, roaming up and down her chest and hips, only to cup her face as he deepened the kiss.

Olivette spread her legs, wanting more. She rocked against him. "Please."

The sound of her voice seemed to bring him from a trance. He stopped moving. "I shouldn't be..."

"You should be," she argued, arching her hips. If he left her now, she felt as if she might wither into nothingness.

The pain had completely dissipated. Pleasure filled her. He drew himself along her opening, so close, but still so hesitant to complete what they'd started.

Mindlessly, she thrust up. He glided inside her, joining their bodies.

She gasped, smiling at the pure ecstasy of the moment. Vitality hummed through her like a drug as they moved in unison.

Their eyes met and locked. Release came in an intense wave, washing over both of them at the same time. She trembled all the way down to her toes. A vibrant energy coursed over her and made her feel invincible. She gasped for breath at the sheer power of it.

Lucius stared down at her as if he too was

amazed by what had happened. He studied her face as if she were fine art in a gallery.

He opened his mouth to speak, but a loud, insistent knock interrupted his words.

"It's all right," she said when he glanced apologetically toward the opened bedroom door and back again. The knock came from somewhere else in the house. "A king's duty is never done."

"Don't leave," he instructed with a quick kiss on her lips.

She gave a small laugh. Even if she had somewhere to go, her body was so relaxed she doubted she could move.

Lucius pulled his tunic shirt over his head as he walked from the bedroom. Muffled voices drifted in. Curious, she sat up to listen.

"*Body...by the...Olym...*"

Olivette pulled the thin yellow covers with her and wrapped it like a dress as she crept toward the doorway.

A man was speaking, "Aye, we're sure. Lady Maia is dead."

"Dead?" Lucius' voice sounded strained. "But that is not possible. What happened? Did the guard worm attack her in the water like it did Pirene?"

The man didn't readily answer.

"Rigel, speak. What happened to Maia?" the king demanded.

"She was found outside the palace gate. They left her," Rigel answered.

"Maia...I can't believe—"

"There is more," Rigel interrupted. "She was not whole."

"You mean...?"

"Yes. They cut her into pieces and left her in two baskets. They made sure she could never recover from her wounds."

Olivette covered her mouth to keep sound from escaping. She didn't wish to be discovered eavesdropping.

Lucius' former lover was dead? The Olympian who did horrible things to humans? Wasn't that a good thing?

"This is distressing news." Lucius' voice lowered, and she had to slide across to the other side of the doorway to hear him.

"What do you think it means?" Rigel asked. "Do you think the Olympians want back into the fold and they are giving us a peace offering?"

"No. I think this is their way of letting me know there is a new queen in the ocean. Lotis is making a point. She wants us to know she has the stomach for war. It's a challenge, a threat."

Olivette leaned forward to get a peek at the two men. Lucius swore as he slapped his hand against a marble wall.

Rigel didn't flinch as he watched the king. The man had dark hair and was smaller in build, but like all the men she'd seen since arriving, he appeared healthy. "Then it is as Lady Victoria discovered from her time with them. Lotis planned to overthrow Queen Maia and is taking over the Olympian cult."

"Where is she now?"

Rigel's eyes found Olivette and his lips pressed together, not answering. He didn't speak, but his body moved as if he did.

The king acted in turn before glancing in her direction. She didn't bother to hide.

They carried on in their strange fashion for a moment before the king nodded to his friend in agreement. He touched him lightly on the shoulder. "Very well, I will meet your brother by the back entrance."

"Maia is dead?" Olivette came from her poorly chosen hiding spot.

"There is nothing for you to be concerned about." Lucius moved past her to grab his pants from the bed. He slipped them on. "You are safe in the palace, and there is no safer place here than in my home."

His eyes didn't meet hers except to glance in her direction a few times as if gauging where she was in the room. When he made his way toward the door, she said, "I'm sorry for your loss."

The words hardly seemed adequate, they never did, but it's what people said to show they cared.

Lucius gestured toward several trays of food. "Please, eat." And with that, he was gone.

8

Lucius turned away from the sight of his ex-lover. It had been years since he'd spared her a kind thought, but seeing her at such an end still affected him. She was an evil sea witch, who on some level probably deserved what happened to her. Still, Lucius would never have ordered such a brutal execution.

A sick feeling built inside of him, like this might be the beginning of the end of his world. Maia had been next to him when they were cast down. Her dark hair pulling away from her head was one of the few things he remembered in detail from that night. He'd held her hand for much of that first swim. Hers was the first words he'd heard clearly in his head, a single voice in a sea of screaming chaos.

Even then, he did not love her. They were joined by something much baser—fear and determination. He did not want to be alone. She wanted to be queen.

"Bury her," Lucius ordered. It had been so long since he'd seen a corpse, and then it had been people they'd tried to save from the top. When that happened, they brought the bodies back to the top in hopes that their families may find and bury their dead. "Quietly. We don't need to cause a panic and a pyre will be too obvious."

"She was set on display," Brutus stated. "The palace guards saw her, as well as workers coming to the palace from the village. I'm not sure this can be contained."

"And no one noticed the mermaids approaching?" the king questioned. "How did a cart simply appear before the palace with no one stopping it?"

"Electra," Brutus stated. "The temptress lulled the guards around to the side of the castle and left them tied. When we discovered the body, we sent scouts to check the palace and found them."

No more explanation was needed.

Electra had been a lovely singer in her mortality, entrancing people to tears with her gift. In immortality, that gift took a dangerous turn. Simply singing a person's name would cause them to lose all will but the one she gave them.

"Electra," the king said after a long pause. "Of course."

He again looked at Maia, forcing himself to see her even as the dread and nausea rose in his throat. It was not lost on him that the moment he'd taken a new lover, his old one was discovered dead. What message from the gods was this? A consequence? As much as he wanted to believe that Poseidon forgot about his lost sea children, Lucius had made that mistake before and they'd been cast down.

Was Olivette his path to redemption? Or was she a temptation he must resist? Was this a test to see if he had learned his lesson, if his royal vanity to satisfy his own needs, to be the hero to his people, had changed?

"My king?" Brutus said, his tone indicating he'd been trying to get Lucius' attention. "It has been a long time since we had a Merr death on land, but are you sure we should not follow the old rituals? If she arrives in Hades' kingdom without at least a basic funeral, this could displease the gods, especially his brothers Poseidon and Zeus. It might indicate we have stopped respecting them again."

"Her followers left her here. There are no relatives to tend her." Lucius knew Brutus was right. If the gods were watching, not performing the funeral would be a mistake. "I hate to ask, especially with Maia in this state, but do you think the hunters' wives will take on the role of her family and help see her safely to the Underworld? I don't know what other females to ask. Althea won't touch the dead."

"I will speak to them. I am sure they will assist in any way they can," Brutus said. "Do we even remember how to do this properly?"

Lucius gave a small laugh.

"What?" Brutus glanced around, trying to see what amused the king.

"Ask Aidan. If anyone would know, it would be him." Lucius took a sheet and drew it over the body. A strand of Maia's hair poked out from beneath.

"Of course. The one man in Ataran who was not here when we were cast down." Brutus gestured that he thought Lucius should leave. Loudly, he ordered, "Gaius, you're to stay by this door and let no one enter. Vitus will have to make do without you."

"Aye, my lord," Gaius agreed. He was newly promoted to guarding the surfacing area after one of the guards died in the ocean during an Olympian attack, but he was not new to the palace. He could be trusted.

Lucius walked in silence next to Brutus through the hall. He'd come this way countless times before, but he looked around as if it were the first. His eyes followed the tiles, seeing the tiniest of irregularities in the pattern. They led to a mosaic of a mermaid under water. Black hair floated around her head. The green eyes weren't quite right, but it could have been Maia. The green of her fins and tail matched the porcelain eyes.

"I am glad to hear your ward is recovering," Brutus said, also observing the mural.

"I see you've spoken to Rigel."

"He mentioned it," Brutus admitted. "He said you both looked...comfortable."

"I haven't stood here to appreciate the details for years," Lucius said, taking the conversation away from Olivette. He wasn't sure what to think about what had happened between them. "I could name every mural and statue in every hallway, but I haven't stopped to look at them for a very long time. What do you think this place looks like to the women when they arrive?"

"My wife said it looks like a museum," Brutus offered. Laurel hadn't been in Atlantes long. "Beautiful and untouchable."

"Antiquated," Lucius whispered. "We live for so

long, things stop changing. Do you remember when we were building this palace, planning the city? There were so many questions and decisions. It gave us something to focus on. And when we finished, we planned the wall outside the palace. And when that was done, we made vases, and the giant mermaid statue in the middle of town. Then we built the hunters' homes in the country."

"And a fine job we did," Brutus agreed.

"Why did we stop building and planning? We created such beauty, and then we stopped as if there was no more to do."

"What would you have us do? Make statues to leave around the bottom of the ocean for the fish?" Brutus touched the edge of the mermaid's tail, tracing the design. "I suppose we had to stop at some point. We had to become complacent and just live. How else are we to get through an eternity? First, we fought for sanity, then we looked for answers, then we grew restless, and finally we accepted our fates."

"That is what concerns me. We have peace..." Lucius glanced toward where Maia's body lay. "We mostly have peace. The Merr people have accepted this life. They know it, understand it. They don't live in fear."

"You're not worried because of Maia, are you?"

Brutus leaned against the mural and turned his attention fully to the king.

"I breathed the surface air, and it tingled but it didn't hurt and it didn't kill me. What happens if we have the cure? What if we can float to the surface and live? What if we have a choice?" Lucius glanced down the palace hall, envisioning the valley below. So many people lived and worked there. "I am their king. It is my responsibility to protect them. That is all I know how to be. Up there, what will happen to our community?"

What will happen to me? he thought. *What am I if not their king?*

"Who knows what the gods will reveal," Brutus said. "All I know is they have blessed me with a wife and I thank them every day for it, and I will do everything in my power to keep her safe."

Lucius thought of the woman he'd left in his home. The memory of her was imprinted on his body. He wanted her again, to feel his heart beat fast and the life pumping through his veins.

Brutus patted him hard on the back, interrupting his thoughts. "I see the gods have blessed you as well, my king."

9

"As promised, new garments." King Lucius smiled as he handed a pile of clothing to Olivette.

She wasn't as quick to return the expression. This was not what she'd been expecting when he returned. The man just found out his old lover had been chopped into pieces and he was bringing her clothing?

"I know it is not the full twenty I promised you, but there are more to come."

Olivette had a sinking feeling as she placed the garments on the couch to get a better look at them. Pinching a dress at the shoulders, she lifted it between them, holding it high enough to hide her stunned expression from his view. It was slutty Mrs.

Claus, only in pale green with bird feathers around the hems instead of fuzzy white.

She turned her attention to the rest of the pile and found...slutty blue, slutty orange, slutty purple...

"Ah..." She tried to think of something to say.

"I am sorry your original gown was ruined, but I hope you can accept these as a replacement." Lucius went to the pile and held up the blue version. Instead of white puffs of material, it had stringy yarn-like yellow.

"I..." Olivette tried to swallow her growing concern. He couldn't be serious, could he? The expression on his face said he was. "I, ah, I can't..."

"Aye, you can accept it. I promised you I would give you the gowns and—"

"When did you promise that?" she questioned, sure she would have remembered such a conversation.

"When I held you in the shower after the dive." Lucius held the dress against his body and smoothed it as if readying it for her use. "You may not remember, but I did promise to give you twenty gowns since yours was ruined, and I always keep my word."

"Oh, dear." She slowly lowered the green gown and placed it on the couch with the others. "This isn't necessary. That wasn't even my dress. It was a work costume."

"But..." He slowly laid the blue dress on the others. He appeared so forlorn.

"Thank you," she said belatedly. "These five gowns are too generous. Please don't make twenty of them. Though, I would like to blend in a little more with the women of Atlantes. Perhaps I could have a gown like Althea in place of the others?"

Lucius smiled. "Aye, my lady. Whatever you wish." He looked at the gowns, and then expectantly at the white floor-length pajama dress she wore.

Olivette forced a smile as she pulled the dressing gown over her head and laid it on the bed. She then reached for the purple gown and tried to slip into it. The fit was snug, just like the original uniform had been. It hung to mid-thigh.

Lucius looked her over before digging to the bottom of the pile. He handed her a pair of leggings. "They are trying to recreate the fishing net you wore, but hopefully these will suffice until then."

Thank the gods for small favors, she thought as she pulled the leggings over her bare legs. At least her ass wouldn't be hanging out as she walked around the palace. Maybe if she were lucky, no one would see her like this.

"Aye, the gods have blessed us," Lucius said with a nod as if he'd read her thoughts.

"Thank you," she said, unsure of what else to say.

"You are beautiful." Lucius cupped her face. "May I kiss you?"

Olivette forgot all about the dress as she looked up at him and nodded. "Yes."

His lips gently met hers. He took his time as he explored the texture of her mouth. When he pulled away, he said, "Someone approaches."

She didn't hear anything.

"Sounds like Aidan's footsteps," the king added. He gave her arms a small squeeze before striding toward the front door. It opened before Aidan had a chance to knock. "Are the arrangements being made?"

"Althea told me the rituals that must be performed, but she will not go near the dead. Ladies Laurel, Lyra, and Victoria are willing. Lady Cassandra is with her husband in the borderlands. Lady Bridget said you had her working on something and she did not think she could stop. Will three be enough?"

"It will have to be," Lucius said.

"Four would be better." Aidan leaned to look at Olivette where she watched them, almost expectantly. By the easy manner in which he spoke to the king, she assumed him to be a trusted advisor of some sort.

Lucius began to shake his head in denial.

"If I can be of help..." Olivette started to offer.

"Aye," Aidan answered.

"No," Lucius said at the same time.

"My lady, thank you," Aidan finished. "Another set of hands would be appreciated."

"I don't think this task is right for," Lucius hesitated, "for someone so new to the abyss."

"The other women are new to the abyss," Aidan said. "Relatively speaking."

Olivette didn't know what she was signing up for, but she wanted to prove herself useful—especially if she was going to be spending time with the king. She could see the tension in Lucius' shoulders. "I'd be happy to be useful."

"No," Lucius stated. "Not this. You don't know what you're agreeing to."

"I don't mind helping if—" she began.

"No," Lucius repeated.

It had been a very long time since someone had treated her like a child and tried to boss her around. She didn't like it. "Oh, but it's fine for the others?

Tell me, does this mean I'm better than them, or worse?"

Lucius looked as if he wanted to argue. His bright blue eyes hardened. Finally, he answered through clenched teeth, "As my lady wishes. Go with Aidan to tend the body."

Olivette began to smile in victory—until his words sank in. Tend the body? This task had something to do with Maia, his ex-lover? She liked pretty things—floral arrangements and well-maintained gardens—not chopped-up dead bodies.

Aidan lifted his hand and motioned that she should follow. She wanted to run in the opposite direction, but it was too late. She had insisted on being useful. Why couldn't she just keep her mouth shut?

Somehow, she managed to make her feet move. She gave a sideways glance up at Lucius as she passed him. He wasn't pleased. She wished for him to grab her arm and demand she not go. He was king and she couldn't defy the order. He didn't move. She listened for footsteps, hoping he would come with her, but the decisive thud of his closing door indicated she was on her own.

"Your help is much appreciated," Aidan said as if

he didn't notice her extreme distress at their current task.

"What exactly am I helping to do?" The words were quiet, maybe too quiet, because he merely glanced at her and didn't directly answer the question.

"That is a lovely dress," Aidan said. "I'm glad to see the king find someone."

"I'm his ward," Olivette answered. "He bought it for me because my other dress was ruined."

"I've heard that before, yet somehow all wards end up being something more to the men who rescued them. I think it's a direct blessing from the gods."

"You're new here, yet you believe in their gods? Is that what you mean when you said you have converted?"

"I've seen too much not to believe. After all, here we are, sunken in the ocean on a lost island of Merr." He gestured to the halls. "Look around, listen to the people you meet, you will begin to see it too within the stories they tell."

Olivette didn't have an answer. She always believed there was more to the world than could be known with modern logic. Though, she had thought those supernatural things would be ghosts or aliens. Ghosts because the energy from a body would presumably transfer at the time of death and had to go somewhere. Aliens because it was a vanity to think they were the only living creatures created in the whole expanse of space. But mermen in the ocean? They had never even blipped in her imagination.

"I don't know what beliefs you hold," Aidan said, "but here, the preparation of the body is a sign of respect the gods demand. The shade, or spirit, began its journey to the Underworld with the last breath, leaving the body in a small gasp of air."

"So I'm playing the part of an undertaker?" She gave a small shiver. Why didn't she just hide in the bedroom and say nothing?

"This really is about pleasing the gods," Aidan said. "We have not sent one of our own to the Underworld for a long time. There was another death, Pirene, but the guard worm ate her so there was no body for a funeral. It's important this is done right, or we will cause insult. We do not wish to fall out of favor, if we are in any kind of favor at all, with Poseidon and his brothers."

"Naturally," she mumbled in half sarcasm, half disbelief.

"From what Althea has explained, there are

three steps to a burial—the *prosthesis,* the *ekphora,* and the interment." Aidan gestured that she should turn the corner. "First, you clean and prepare the body with oils. Then, afterward you'll carry it to the grave at dawn. And, finally, you'll place it into the ground and cover it. It won't be much of a procession to the gravesite, as they're trying to keep the death..." Aidan stopped as if he realized how loud he was talking and lowered his voice to a whisper. "We're trying to keep the death quiet."

"Why?" she asked, just as softly. They passed a mural of a red octopus sitting near a shipwreck.

"I..." He looked back toward the king's home. "I am not sure I can tell you."

"You want me to tend a dead body and you don't think you can tell me why?" Olivette arched a brow and looked the man over. He wanted to tell her. She could see the need to speak bubbling inside of him. "I already know it's Maia."

"You know?" he asked in surprise. "That's a relief. Maia wasn't well liked, but her death means something is happening with the Olympians. There is a power shift."

If she wasn't mistaken, Aidan sounded almost excited by this.

"Is that a good thing?"

"It depends." Aidan again gestured her to turn a corner. "If they revolted because they want to rejoin the Merr under King Lucius' rule, then yes."

"But you don't think that's what this is?" Olivette paused by the mural of a mermaid under water. She lightly touched the tiles as she passed, shivering at the idea of someday growing her own fish tail.

"I think it's more likely a power struggle," Aidan admitted. He touched the mermaid picture briefly. "Everything I've heard about Queen Maia and her followers leads me to believe they're not the type to admit they were wrong and seek forgiveness. That is why you must bury Maia quietly but properly."

"Sounds straightforward," Olivette said, still not wanting to participate.

"Oh, hell no!" A woman gagged as she stumbled into the hall and covered her mouth. The golden brown of her hair was pulled into a messy bun on the top of her head. She shook her head violently in denial at no one in particular.

"Lady Laurel?" Aidan questioned, leaving Olivette by the mural to rush to Laurel's side. "What is it? What happened?"

"I'm not rubbing oil on that," Laurel declared, gagging a second time. "Have you seen what's in there?"

A second woman joined the first. She covered her nose and mouth with her hands, nearly hiding her green eyes with her fingertips. Her long dark blonde hair was tied at the nape of her neck and whipped as she came to an abrupt stop. The words were muffled as she said, "It smells like a fish cannery in there. The king has lost his fucking mind. He can't be serious about this."

"Lady Lyra, please," Aidan begged, with a glance at Olivette.

Both women turned to look at her. Their eyes moved over her attire, and she glanced down self-consciously. She still wore the costume.

"This mermaid tried to kill me at least three times." A third woman joined the group, appearing to have a stronger stomach than the others. "I can't say I'm sorry she's no longer a threat."

"Lady Victoria." Aidan acknowledged the brunette. "Lyra, Laurel, please, I'd like to introduce you to Olivette. She's here to help—"

"Fresh meat," Lyra stated, rubbing her hands together.

"Ignore her," Laurel waved in dismissal of her friend. "She's only teasing."

Lyra's smile didn't look threatening.

"Welcome to Atlantes," Victoria said. "I'm newly

arrived myself, but if there's anything I can do to make your transition easier, please let me know."

"Thank you," Olivette said. "That's very kind of you."

"Olivette, that's a pretty name," Laurel said.

"I'm told it means elf army," Olivette answered. The women began to chuckle.

"That explains the outfit." Lyra motioned to Olivette's clothes.

Aidan looked at Olivette's clothes. "What's wrong with the outfit?"

"I'm a purple Mrs. Claus minus a stripper pole," Olivette mumbled.

The women laughed harder. Lyra moved toward her, only to hook her arm around her shoulders. "I like you, elf."

"Ladies," Aidan insisted. "About your duties—"

"Take it easy, Aidan, we got your ancient ritual. We'll come find you when we're done," Victoria said.

Lyra led Olivette back the way the women had come. "Hold your breath, elf, this is going to be a long night."

10

Long didn't even begin to describe the night Olivette had. After preparing Maia the best they could, taking shifts when the task became too difficult, they carried the dead queen on a cot through the back door of the palace. Victoria insisted on a shroud. It was for the best as the mermaid was hard to look at.

Torches lit the halls and greeted them as they stepped into the dark outdoors. Olivette took several deep breaths of air, only to gasp as the king stepped out of the darkness to join them. He glanced at the shrouded body before nodding at the woman. He moved ahead of them, leading the small procession. The other women's husbands also joined them, each carrying a torch—Lyra's Rigel, Laurel's Brutus, and Victoria's Demon.

Yes, the woman's husband was actually named Demon. And aptly so. He looked like a giant brute of a man with long black hair and black eyes, as did his identical twin, Brutus. Rigel was their younger brother, a lighter version of the twins with dark brown hair and gray eyes.

The king led them from the palace down a dirt path. She willed him to turn around and look at her, but the rigid set of his back said he would not. Perhaps she'd read too much into their time together. She'd been the one to seduce him after all.

Olivette couldn't help looking up to see the dome of her new world. Stars danced overhead, swimming in gentle patterns. She could detect no dome, but saw the bioluminescent creatures part as dark streaks tore through them. Had she not seen the trip down for herself, she might have questioned it.

"Hey, elf," Lyra whispered.

Olivette realized she'd stopped walking and her corner of the cot had slipped out of her hands. She hurried to catch up. At the sound, the king did glance back at them. His eyes met hers. She tried to mouth an apology, but he turned away too quickly.

The women had told her that a village was on the

front side of the palace, but where they walked looked abandoned. Tree roots reached up from the ground to create strange mossy arches over the land, and the branches stretched like creepy fingers over their heads. It was within the silent forest that King Lucius turned, leading them toward a shadowed clearing. Such scenes were the thing cult movies were made of. Men and women in ancient-inspired garb circling a large stone altar as a dead woman was placed on top.

Then there was Olivette, a stranger who did not belong in her ridiculous elf attire, a misplaced jingle bell of a brightly colored spot during the solemn affair. She stepped back to the edge of light, watching as Lucius kneeled before the altar. He placed small pieces of food on the stone before stepping away. The hunters lifted the cot and lowered it into a hole, not bothering to remove the transport as they buried Maia beneath scoops of dirt.

After the dirt was in place, the men picked up the altar and moved it on top of the mound, hiding the disturbed earth beneath the stone. It was as if Maia had never been. The food was left on the altar. The king stood, staring at it as the hunters led their wives out of the clearing. Olivette wasn't sure if she should stay or follow. She watched the king, hearing the soft rustle of retreating footsteps. When he didn't ask her to stay, she made a move to catch up with the others.

"Very few come to this old altar," the king said, stopping her. "She will never be discovered here."

Olivette turned around to meet his gaze. She waited for him to say more, unsure how to provide comfort. It was not like in his home when the physical need of her body to heal drew her to him in mesmerizing passion. This moment carried more weight, more logic, more doubt. She wanted to comfort him but had the presence of mind to hold back.

"I'm sorry for your loss," she said, unsure what else to say. "I can't imagine this is easy for you, even if you did say you two were not in touch for many years."

"I was thinking of the beginning when we first came down. Maia had been with me before the ground began to quake, and then she found me in the water. There was so much confusion and fear. I never forgot it. It flooded into me, their screams and panic as we changed for the first time. We didn't understand what telepathy was and it added to the chaos. For some reason, Maia didn't scream, not like the others. It was as if she understood the curse and didn't care. Maybe I remember it wrong after all these years. I saw fear in her, I know that. We were all scared but she accepted it."

Olivette moved closer to him. She placed a gentle hand on his arm. He continued to stare at her, but his eyes didn't appear to see her.

"The day she left the palace, she told me I was a fool. She said I had declared us gods on Earth and the gods answered by giving us immortality. What I called a curse, she called a blessing. She told me I wasted that gift in self-loathing and pining for a surface life, and that I did not deserve to be king."

"Maybe you were both wrong," Olivette said. "Maybe it's not a curse or a blessing. Maybe it just is."

At that, he blinked several times and focused his renewed attention on her, as if coming out of the past.

"I think sometimes people read too much meaning into the world around them, always looking for signs. Sometimes bad things happen. Sometimes good things happen. I'm here because an asshole tried to rape me and then threw me over the side of a boat to hide his drunken mistake. That was bad. I was able to meet Laurel, and Lyra, and Victoria, and I consider that a good thing as they seem like very nice people. Though, how I met them wasn't exactly a pleasant circumstance." She glanced at the grave marker. "Maybe Poseidon didn't curse you. Maybe he simply wanted more sea creatures."

He followed her gaze to the altar and stared at it.

"But what do I know? I've only been here less than a week." She dropped her hand from him and stepped away. As much as she wanted to hold him, she realized that she was speaking to a king.

Why hadn't she stopped to consider that fact? A king. He ruled the entirety of her new home. Well, except for a few rebels. He had power and position. What did she think was going to happen if she pursued a relationship with him? He'd fall in love with her and she'd become his queen? She didn't want that kind of power or responsibility. The fate of an entire country did not need to rest in her hands, not even in part.

Or did she want to be his lover? Olivette turned again to the grave. Things had not turned out too well for the last woman who'd held the position.

"And meeting me?" he asked. "Do you consider that to be a good or bad thing?"

"I'm grateful to be alive." She knew her answer was evasive as it came out but what else could she say? If she allowed herself to feel the way she was feeling about him, then she was choosing a future that she didn't want. She wanted Lucius but doubted simple emotion was enough. She didn't want to be a queen or to be known as the lover of a king. She didn't want the spotlight or power. She wanted to create and spread beauty in the world.

Her task today had not been beautiful.

"Thank you for helping out this morning," he said.

She glanced up, but trees blocked the dancing stars. "Is it morning?"

"When the sea stars begin to disappear, and the light shifts. It's as much of a dawn as we will see. It is the best we can do to honor the dead." Lucius tapped the altar gently before walking away from the site.

Olivette followed him. "Please let me know if you'd like to talk. I know this must be a difficult time for you."

He bowed his head but didn't stop walking. "I said goodbye to Maia long ago. She made her choices. What I feel is not grief over her loss, but grief over all our losses, and the reminder of mortality for the immortal. You cannot understand the passage of time, not until you have lived for thousands of years with its ravishes and whims."

11

OLIVETTE WAS AN IDIOT. She should have just kissed Lucius that night by the gravesite. She should have held him and walked beside him. She should have kissed him the next morning, and the morning after that one. Instead, she'd kept a wall between them, not allowing herself to respond to his understated advances. And he was too respectful to make more than subtle hints.

She was an idiot—an edgy, grumpy idiot.

Fine, mostly she was horny. Seriously, the ache she felt every time Lucius was near only grew worse by the moment. If he bothered to touch her arm, she'd probably orgasm and make an embarrassment of herself.

Now it was too late. She'd woken up a few nights

ago to find he had left the palace for the forest with no word as to when he'd return.

So, here she was, three weeks after the funeral, following Lyra into town to meet Cassandra, another surface woman. For some reason, Lyra preferred to take a side entrance out of the palace. They followed the long wall surrounding the palace. Bright yellow lines accented blue stones. Like inside, the outside walls depicted sea creatures. They led to a narrow gate that let them slip beyond the inner courtyard.

The one good thing was, Lyra had given her a dress that didn't look like it belonged in Santa's slutty kingdom. She was glad to be in something that didn't have a fluffy hemline and stockings.

The dark blue sky looked nothing like the surface, yet light shone as if she stood in the sunlight. They heard the faint sounds of the village before Atlas actually came into view. The town was settled in a valley beyond the main gate. The grid-like roads were measured to perfect lengths, surrounding a circular clearing of the town center. Since they didn't have motor vehicles or horse-drawn carriages, there were only cobblestone roads for pulling carts and walking. The homes were packed together on each block with no yards or alleyways between.

"Not handling the transition down very well, are you?" Lyra broke their long silence.

Olivette blinked in surprise and shook her head in slight denial. "What makes you say that?"

"You've been glaring at the palace wall since we walked outside," Lyra observed. "I'm not judging. I gave my husband a run for his money when I came down. I'm glad I finally let him catch me, but I do like keeping him on his toes."

Olivette's lip curled, as she thought, *Yeah, yeah, keep bragging. You have a wonderful, perfect relationship and I'm an idiot.*

"And there's the look again," Lyra said. "I know I can be a little abrasive sometimes. Did I say something to piss you off?"

"Lucius left and I don't know when he's coming back." She wasn't sure why she admitted it, but she liked Lyra.

"Ah, understood." Lyra nodded. "Well, I would assume soon. I received word from my husband that they're tracking the Olympians and hope to catch up to them shortly."

"Word?" Olivette grabbed Lyra's arm in concern. "Did someone deliver a message? Are they safe? Is it too late to send a message back? From everything I've heard of the Olympians, that doesn't sound safe."

"You do know about the telepathy, don't you? I spoke to my husband through our mind link. It's harder to do when he's far away, but we manage to get fragmented messages to each other."

"Oh," Olivette said. "I don't have that."

"You haven't gone through the transformation yet," Lyra said. "I can't say I blame you. Drowning is hard enough. Choosing to drown so you can become a mermaid is a terrifying choice to make."

"Does it hurt?"

Lyra opened her mouth. It looked as if she wanted to lie, but in the end, she sighed and nodded. "Drowning? Yes. Transforming? No. Turning into a mermaid is more like pinpricks. Once it's over though, it's worth it."

Olivette swallowed nervously. She wasn't sure she could ever choose to drown. "How many Merr are there in Atlantes?"

"I'm not sure. I'm told that very few actually live in town. Many have homes in the country. If I had to guess, I'd say a few thousand." Lyra hooked her arm through Olivette's. "You'll notice that most of them appear to be between the ages of twenty-five and forty. I'm sure it has something to do with the life expectancy back in the ancient times. You also won't see children, except for Bridget's triplets."

"So that's why everything is so clean and pretty." Olivette let Lyra lead her down the hillside to town.

"What do you mean?"

"Kids are messy. I worked as a temp in a daycare for about a month." Olivette chuckled. "It took me three hours to clean what it would take them two minutes to destroy."

Lyra's smile was sad. "I probably wouldn't joke about kids here. It's a very sensitive subject."

"I don't understand." Olivette furrowed her brow before realizing what Lyra meant. "You're saying they can't have children, not that they chose not to have more?"

Lyra nodded. "Rigel wants a child. He doesn't complain, but I know he secretly wishes for one. Bridget and Caderyn were special. She was the only one to become pregnant. You should see King Lucius with those boys. He spoils them terribly. If you watch, though, when the boys are playing, you'll see the heartache in the men's eyes, the longing."

"I'm sorry. I didn't mean to make light of—"

"You didn't know," Lyra said. "I didn't take offense at anything you said. But you are right. This place is beautiful. Have you seen the mermaid statue in the town center?"

"No." Olivette shook her head in denial.

"Come on. There are some shops I want to take you to near there. I've been trying to work with the bakery to make cinnamon rolls. Sadly, we don't have cinnamon so it's been difficult, but they're getting closer."

Olivette tried to smile at those they passed. Some waved. Others watched curiously. None approached.

"They're not sure what to make of you," Lyra explained. "Since you were found by Lucius, there are rumors that you will be his..."

"Lover?" Olivette supplied when she didn't finish her sentence.

"Queen," Lyra corrected.

The woman's words only made her nervous, like she was being judged.

"There." Lyra pointed as they came to the town center.

Olivette's breath caught as she looked up at the beautiful statue of a mermaid. A long tail swept behind the woman's naked torso. Every scale was carved to reveal the movement of muscle beneath, stone hair looked as if it flowed in the air, and the tail fin had been lined in perfect detail. Even the mermaid's nipples stood erect as if brushed by cold water.

"Amazing, right?" Lyra prompted.

"Stunning," Olivette whispered. "The detail."

"I'll be in the bakery over there," Lyra said. "Join me when you're ready."

Olivette glanced at the shops. Someone had started an intricate tapestry on a tapestry loom. Next to her was a man blowing glass, his hands moving with such precision as if the task took no thought on his part. One building had a carved fish, so she assumed it was a butcher shop. Lyra entered a narrow door—the bakery.

"You must be Olivette."

Olivette turned at the sound. It was the first townsperson to speak to her. The woman had bright red hair and playful green eyes.

"Let me guess, Lyra is after her cinnamon rolls again," the redhead chuckled. "I told her, you can't make cinnamon out of seaweed and hope, but she is determined."

"Yes, I'm Olivette," she said belatedly.

"Cassandra, nice to meet you." Cassandra held out her hand for Olivette to shake. "What part of the surface are you from?"

"Florida," she said.

"Our boat left from Florida." Cassandra glanced up. "Bridget and I were on a scientific vessel."

"I was murdered by a psychopathic aide to a politician," Olivette said.

Cassandra arched a brow. "Interesting. I hope the scylla wrecked his boat for you."

"No. As far as I know, he's still up there." Olivette wondered where Tanner was now. Did anyone even notice she was gone yet?

"Try not to think about it," Cassandra said. "The unanswerable questions will only drive you crazy. My husband, Iason, helped me find a way to communicate with Lyra's family on the surface. They're all men of the sea, so she knew where to find them. If you have any requests, she can ask them to send it down. Lyra, naturally, wants cinnamon. Or if you have loved ones, she can try to send word to the surface for you."

"Jason?" Olivette asked, not thinking she'd heard the woman right.

"No, *Iason*. It's the Ancient Greek version of the name," Cassandra said. "Have you met Demon?"

Olivette nodded.

"That name threw me for a loop. I never realized people named their kids that. Anyway, let me know if you think of anything you need," Cassandra offered again. "Communication has become incredibly fast. I contact them about twice a year now and it only takes them a few months to answer. We go out again in a few weeks."

"There is one letter I'd like to write. Thank you." Olivette thought of the man who'd thrown her overboard. If no one realized or cared that she was missing, she'd make sure someone noticed—like a news outlet. Let them take a closer look at Mr. Tanner Tapert's life. She couldn't have been the only woman he'd ever attacked.

"Cass, Elf, come try this with me," Lyra yelled.

"Elf?" Cassandra asked.

"Don't ask."

"Oh, I have to now." Cassandra moved toward Lyra. "Why do you call her Elf?"

Lyra chuckled and pointed toward a shop across the way. "Because she inspired the new fashion trend."

"Oh, no!" Cassandra laughed so hard she had to grab her stomach. "What is that monstrosity?"

Olivette leaned over to see where they looked. What appeared to be a dressmaker's shop had three versions of her elf attire in the window on display, presumably for sale to the local women.

"We have to get one," Cassandra exclaimed. "It's too hilarious not to."

As if by divine intervention, the weaver came out

of her shop wearing a bright yellow version of the Mrs. Claus costume. Olivette's words were lost as she coughed in surprise. The weaver smiled at them as she went to work on her loom.

"Fine, but first you need to come try these new concoctions with me." Lyra moved back inside the bakery.

Olivette couldn't help but laugh as she made a move to join the women inside. To herself, she mumbled, "I guess I did contribute something to this society after all."

Lucius pushed through the underwater tunnels, not wanting to admit that he was lost in the maze. It was worse than they could have ever imagined. The Olympians must have spent decades mining the underground routes to the ocean. No wonder they kept appearing each time the hunters managed to block one of their tunnels.

The darkness did not bother him as he was used to seeing through the dark waters of the ocean. What worried him was the instability of several tunnels they passed. Passages were blocked by a rock fall. The smell of decay in the water caused him to stiffen and slow his pace. He inched along a fractured tunnel, only to find a skeletal arm poking out from the rocks. By the length of the fin it looked to be a male. Someone had dulled the edge of the fin to keep it from cutting. One of the Olympian slaves, perhaps?

'*Maia, what were you doing?*' Lucius said, more to himself than anyone else.

'*My king?*' Brutus' voice filled his mind. '*Come this way. We found a path out. These tunnels are not sturdy. One almost caved in on Demon.*'

'*The Olympians are not in here,*' Demon added. '*Even they must know what they created is not safe.*'

'*No wonder the guard worm has been territorial of late. They've been invading his home within the rock dome,*' Lucius said. '*It explains why it attacked and killed Pirene.*'

The land above him began to tremor, vibrating the water within the tunnels. Lucius heard rocks falling behind him.

'*Hurry,*' Brutus yelled. '*They're caving in!*'

Lucius surged forward, pulling with his arms to speed his way through.

'*The integrity is too weak. They did not brace the structure with support beams.*' Iason's voice joined theirs. He'd found a tunnel entry while with his wife, Cassandra, in the country. '*Follow my vibrations. I'm out in the ocean.*'

The steady tap of a hand on the rock was hard to

decipher in the rumbling tunnels, but somehow Lucius managed to emerge from within. Brutus and Demon reached into the tunnel and pulled him out as he swam forward. Rocks continued to clink inside the unsafe hole. The stone pedestal held Atlantes above the ocean floor, allowing it free movement with the currents. What the Olympians had done weakened the base of their home.

'It's almost like they want to destroy the dome.' Lucius scanned the surrounding ocean. Small sea creatures were scrambling away from the dome as if they sensed it was in danger. Their translucent bodies glimmered briefly before disappearing into the sand.

'But why? They need Atlantes as much as we do. Without it, they will be lost to the sea just like the rest of us,' Iason said.

Lucius shared a look with Brutus. The method for breathing surface air came from the Olympians. It was possible the crazy mermaids planned to force everyone in the dome to either bow to them or die. Either way, the mermaids had found a way to survive on the surface.

'I must show you something,' Iason said. His shoulder-length blond hair covered his face as he moved to swim up toward the soft light of the dome.

Lucius followed the movement of his green tail up the rocky incline. The soft glow from within the dome penetrated the darkness. It sat like a frozen bubble trapped in water. So strong, yet appearing so delicate. He touched the smooth surface, letting his hand glide over it. Beyond his hand, on the other side, he saw the trees along the borderland. Though so close, it was impossible to get to through the barrier. Above them, the dome stretched high to create the Atlantean sky.

'Look.' Iason gestured to the barrier. *'Tell me I imagine that.'*

Lucius swam to where he indicated.

A small crack had formed in the dome, a thin thread reaching from the rock base and fracturing out like three crooked fingers. A tiny air bubble formed along the seam. Lucius touched it lightly with his finger. The bubble skated up the side of the dome.

'The crazy sea witches actually went through with it,' Brutus said.

'We have to seal it,' Demon insisted. *'We must check the entire dome.'*

'Aye.' Lucius nodded. He stared at the crack as if it manifested all his fears from over the centuries below the surface.

His people needed the dome to survive. They

could not survive in the ocean. They'd try, but in the end, all the Merr would succumb to the dark insanity. They would become the thing his people hunted. They would become scylla.

'We can't let this happen,' Iason whispered. 'I would rather die than become a mindless scylla, killing those from the surface world. Imagine, thousands of us roaming the waters. No ship would be safe.'

'The humans won't know how to hunt scylla,' Demon added.

'This can't be happening. We only just found our wives,' Brutus said. 'The gods would not take them from us so soon. What more do they want? What more can we do to please them?'

Lucius stared at the crack. He'd only just found Olivette. For some reason, she hesitated around him even though he felt her desire. He thought to give her time to learn what he knew. But what if they didn't have time? What if this was the end of their world?

'The seaweed,' Brutus said. 'We must make everyone eat the seaweed.'

'We don't know if that works,' Iason disputed.

'It does,' Lucius answered.

'My king?' Iason asked.

'I breathed surface air and lived,' Lucius said.

Iason grabbed his arm and forced him to look at him. *'This news is too important. I would have heard about it.'*

'We were there,' Demon said. *'It's true.'*

'Why you, my king? If it didn't—' Iason protests came weeks too late.

'Because it was his duty as king to lead the way up for his people,' Demon defended, even though he himself had made the same protest when they were making their way toward the surface.

Realizing he gripped the king, Iason let go and swam a few inches back. He searched the king as if looking for injuries. *'And, it worked?'*

'Aye,' Lucius said. *'I breathed the surface air and I lived.'*

'What was it like?' Iason asked.

'It tingled,' Lucius answered, unable to describe it beyond that. He'd seen Olivette falling into the water and the experience of being the first merman to breathe surface air had paled in comparison.

'Look at the fallen king, as he realizes everything he rules is about to crumble.'

Lucius spun around. Lotis held her arms wide and swished her tail as she held her place in the water. She wore a metal crown.

The mermaid reminded him of blood in the

water. Her red hair, eyes, and scales were unlike any other in Atlantes. There was evilness inside her, a diabolical nature that she couldn't hide. It shone in her eyes and revealed itself in the way her lips curled into a smile. She was an empty vessel that some force had filled with every negative substance they could find—hatred, vindictiveness, selfishness, murderous impulses. Add all that to the boredom of centuries and a true sea witch was born.

'Nothing to say?' Lotis taunted. The mermaids Electra and Carmenta swam up behind her in support. Electra seemed to be ever changing, glistening like water in sunlight.

Carmenta was a blonde with purplish-gray fins. He had not remembered her to be a cruel woman, but in truth it had been decades since he's seen her.

'You killed Maia,' Lucius stated. What more was there to say to this woman? She had clearly lost her sanity long ago. Only a madwoman would lay such horror at his doorstep.

'I did.' Lotis said the words with pride.

'You don't even try to deny it,' Iason spat.

'No one is talking to you, peasant.' Lotis glared at Iason.

'Quiet your tongue in front of royalty,' Electra ordered.

Carmenta's expression did not match the others. She glanced at the king and then away.

'*I recognize no queen,*' Iason returned.

'*Surrender now and you will be shown mercy,*' Lucius offered, hoping at least Carmenta would take it. He did not wish to hurt anyone, even these disillusioned women.

'*I was about to say the same thing.*' Lotis' laughter clouded the mind link. '*But we all know you will never bow to a woman.*'

Lucius thought of Olivette.

'*I grow bored with this,*' Lotis stated. '*Deal with them.*'

Mermaids surged from below as if they'd been creeping closer in silence. The ocean became a flurry of blurred movements. The Olympians attacked, trying to slash with their sharp fins to tear the mermen's chests and necks with deadly force. Lucius fought back, joining the hunters as they defended themselves. He knew none of them wanted to hurt the mermaids.

Blood clouded the water. He felt his fin meet flesh. Lucius did not want to kill. He ordered them to surrender through the mind link but they kept coming. He caught Lotis swimming in the background, grinning at the chaos she'd created.

The water began to vibrate. Sea creatures came from the darkness and charged the dome. They had done this once before when Maia had called them to create earthquakes within. But now the dome was cracked. Gigantic squid sacrificed themselves on the barrier, slamming so hard it instantly killed them. They fell to the sea floor, polluting the waters with their death.

Lucius tried to focus his mind on turning the sea creatures back.

Lotis closed her eyes, summoning all she could. A mermaid grabbed his arm and he tried to shake her off as she broke his concentration. Another squid hit the dome.

'*You must stop her,*' Carmenta's voice whispered through the insanity. Her eyes pleaded with him to listen. '*She destroys everything she touches. She won't stop until Atlantes falls—*'

Carmenta's mouth opened as blood spurted from between her lips.

Lotis jerked her fin out of the woman's back. '*Traitor.*'

Lucius pushed Carmenta aside and swept his arm toward Lotis. He met with flesh. Lotis' scream filled his mind as she quickly called a retreat.

He turned to access the damage. The crack had

fractured its way up the side of the dome. He saw air leaking out, bubbling at a faster rate. Lucius wanted to give chase, but another squid came to join the others.

'Turn the creatures,' he ordered. *'The dome won't last.'*

They used the mind link to warn the creature away. The giant squid turned at the last moment, surging and bumping along the dome. The creature barreled through the retreating Olympians, throwing them in every direction. Their screams died, some on impact with the squid, others as they were flung hard onto the rocks below.

Lucius watched a squid dragged Lotis along the dome wall. The animal crushed her repeatedly before it pushed away from the dome and changed direction. Lotis' dead body slid along the dome before dropping once more.

The dome crack had spread at the impact from the squid. Iason swam upward to assess the damage. Lucius darted down to examine the carnage of what had happened. Lotis lay like a broken mass on the ocean floor, her red eyes still open as if they held on to the rage of her life. They had not meant to kill so many as they'd tried to save the dome.

'Water drips in,' Iason reported. 'Air escapes. The crack is spreading in too many directions.'

'What does this mean?' Brutus asked. 'How do we fix it?'

'I don't know that we can,' Iason answered. 'We would have to encase the dome in stone, even then it might not be enough, and who knows if the dome would support the weight.'

'This is the beginning of the end,' Lucius answered. 'The days of Atlantes are numbered. We have no choice but to evacuate the people, and hope that the gods will bless us to walk on the surface world once more.'

The fear they all felt at that moment did not need to be spoken. It flowed in every gesture and look. Lucius saw Lotis' crown caught on a rocky ledge, a strange symbol. Now that the chaos had died down, the scavengers of the abyss began to return, coming for the food left for them from the battle.

'Leave them. They chose their fates. We will send someone back for them if there is time.' Lucius thought of Olivette. Had he saved her from one horrible death, only to condemn her to another? 'Right now, we need to get home.'

Lucius found Olivette standing by the saltwater pool, staring at the surface. She breathed heavily as she contemplated the still water. He imagined he felt the fear coming from her, but it might have been his own.

"You felt the tremors?" he asked as he approached.

Olivette nearly jumped out of her skin at his voice. She gasped sharply and stumbled back from the water. She clutched her hands over her heart.

Lucius stopped walking and held up his hands as if to reassure her from a distance.

Olivette hurried toward him. "You're back. Word came while we were in the village that you were out in the water. Then we saw the dark shadows over the dome and felt the earthquakes. I was trying to..." She gestured to the water. "Lyra told me how Laurel drowned herself in the pool and had Bridget sneak her out into the ocean so that she could help save Brutus."

"You were going to drown yourself to save me?" he asked.

A tear slipped over her cheek. "I tried, but I was scared."

Lucius pulled her into his arms.

"I'm so glad you're not hurt," she whispered before pushing back to look at him. "You're not hurt, are you?"

"No." He held her close once more, not wanting to let her go.

"I'm sorry I'm such an idiot."

"What do you mean?" It was his turn to try to study her face.

Olivette lifted up on her toes and kissed him. Her arms moved around his neck and she kept him from pulling away. Lucius moaned, trying to keep his wits enough to realize they were in the swimming area. He lifted her in his arms and carried her through the halls. The feel of her mouth made him stumble as he made haphazard patterns through the halls instead of walking a straight line.

"My king," Bridget gasped in shock, having caught them making out in the palace halls.

The sound broke them apart long enough for him to correct his course and continue to his home. He hit the door with his shoulder, knocking it open and weakening the latch. He bumped it a second time, forcing it to close and give them privacy.

"I do not find you to be an idiot." Lucius let her feet drop to the ground.

"I'm an idiot for not doing that sooner. I hated it when you went away," she confessed, taking a small step back. "I should have listened to what my heart and body were telling me, not my stupid brain. I want to be with you, Lucius. I know you're not looking for a queen, and I'm all right with that, but I want to be with you. It hurts—actually hurts—when you're not near me. I can't breathe when you're not around. There is an emptiness I can't describe."

"Who says I am not looking for a queen?"

"I thought..." She gestured helplessly at nothing in particular. "After Maia, and well..."

"I love you, Olivette." He closed the small distance between them. "I never loved Maia. I never made her promises. I never felt the connection with her that I have with you. I've known how I've felt since the first time our lips met under the water. It is the Merr way to know the other piece of our heart when we find it. The knowledge may be one of the few blessings the gods gave us. You weren't even conscious then. And later when you kissed me, really kissed me, it cemented my feelings."

"You didn't say anything, didn't let on." She lifted up on her toes and kissed him. A soft moan escaped her lips.

"I didn't want to force you. I imagine coming down here is not easy. I'm sure it can be confusing."

"Yes, it's not exactly easy but I'm not confused." Olivette tugged at his clothing, lifting his shirt so her hands could glide over the flesh at his waist. "When I'm near you, I feel the pull. My wanting to be with you has never been in question."

"Then what is in question?"

Her hands paused in their exploration. "I don't think I'll make a good queen. I know nothing about it. And the position of the king's lover feels like it comes with a little too much public responsibility. Then I went to the dining hall, and to the village. I heard the people talk about you, about this place. I saw the beauty that was created under your rule—that mermaid statue in the village, the palace murals, the carvings on the houses, the vases, and plates, and...everything."

"That is nonsense. You would make a lovely queen." Lucius threw his shirt over his head and reached for her gown. He lifted it from her and tossed it aside. The passion he had for her burned so brightly that it outshone everything else. When he touched her, he knew that this was where he was meant to be. And if his world was going to end, then selfishly, she was who he wanted to be with when it did. However much time the gods gave them, the centuries before would be worth it to have this moment with her. One kiss, that is all he needed to be happy.

Olivette did not know it but she had rule over him. By extension, she had rule over all of Atlantes. He wasn't worried. He knew that they would be safe in her capable hands. He trusted her like he trusted no one. The feeling was both strange and exhilarating. To trust somebody so fully, to know them with such certainty. For all that he believed swimming an eternity in the ocean was a curse, there was one thing about being Merr that gave them an advantage over when they were human. As a shifter, when he knew, he knew. Looking at her, it was incredibly clear. They were meant to be together.

There was so much he wanted to say to her, so much he should tell her. The worry about his people stayed in the back of his mind. But how could he wipe that smile off her face? How could he end this beautiful moment? He wanted it. He needed it. He needed her.

"I love you," he whispered.

Before she could respond, he kissed her again and urged her into the bedroom. Hands roamed over bodies. The more they touched, the more desperate he became. He lifted her briefly and then laid her on the bed. He had to protect her. He had to protect all of them. He drank in the comfort of her mouth, the reassurance of her touch.

He had been without it for so long, and the affliction was so deep, that he had a hard time holding back. Luckily, he did not have to. She was as urgent as he.

Olivette wiggled as he pulled the pants from his hips. There was no hesitation. He surged forward. They joined hard and fast, sliding together as if they were always meant to be. He wanted it to last forever, but the pleasure was too hard to resist. Her body trembled, and he met her release with his own.

Afterward, he rolled back, pulling her next to him on the bed. He held her close in the dim light.

"How do people get married here anyway?" she asked.

"They announce their intentions and I bless the union." He leaned his head back to study her. "Are you asking me to marry you?"

"You know, crazy as it sounds, I think I might be," Olivette giggled.

"Then you have my blessing," he whispered, holding her close. "For what good it's worth."

"What are you not saying?" She touched his face.

"I'm sorry. I brought you here right at the end, and as much as I want you to be my queen, I feel I must tell you what it is you will face."

"Are you changing your mind already?" She frowned.

"I love you, Olivette, have no doubts about that, but as my queen, you join me at our most dire time."

As if to punctuate his words, a tremor shook the room.

"All right. Now you seriously have me worried." She sat up on the bed.

Lucius told her all that had happened, before saying, "Lotis is dead, but before she died, she sealed the fate of this dome."

"How long?"

"Days? A week? We can't be sure. I should have told you the second I came back, but you looked so lovely by the pool. I wanted a moment with you before—"

"Before we come up with a plan to save our people," she inserted firmly. "Either we sit here and accept fate or we do something about it. If people need to eat seaweed to breathe air, then bring on the salads."

"It is already being gathered, and we are calling everyone in from the countryside, or sending them to the Olympian tunnels we discovered. It's not the safest route, but I'm not sure they have three days to get here by land. People will start to arrive at the palace soon, but—"

"No buts." Olivette held up her hand. "I'm from Florida, the land of hurricanes. So we treat this like an oncoming disaster. Best to be prepared. If it doesn't come, great. If it does, we have an emergency plan in place. Make sure people only pack items of importance and what can be carried in the water, and if there is time, we'll go back to secure the rest. People tend to place misguided importance on objects during times of panic. If the dome doesn't hold, then maybe someday someone will come back and find that which is lost."

"Yes. Already you show much wisdom, my queen." Everything about her amazed him.

She stood, looking around the room. "As beautiful as this palace is, these are just things. Life must come first."

Another earthquake hit, lasting longer than the others. Olivette cried out and covered her head. The wall cracked under the disturbance and chunks began to fall in heavy thuds. Lucius tugged her from the bed moments before the wall caved in. It might already be too late.

14

OLIVETTE COUGHED as the dust drifted into the living room from the bedroom She covered her mouth and took several deep breaths. The sound of water trickled loudly. As the tremors stopped, she looked at the ceiling. The outside air filled the room. Water trickled down the side of the wall from a busted pipe.

"We need clothes." Lucius passed her to go back into the bedroom. He tossed a nightgown at her before taking his own tunic and pants. As he made a move to leave, his feet hit the puddle of water and he slipped.

Olivette cried out as she went to catch him. His legs slid in the water, the skin transforming with scales and his feet half-shifted to fins.

Lucius touched the puddle and lifted his hand to see it also transformed. "Saltwater."

They both looked up.

"That's not a busted pipe," she whispered.

"The dome is breaking," he said.

Fear filled her, reflected in his gaze. She grabbed his arm and pulled him from the wet rubble. When they were out of the bedroom, she let go and tugged the gown over her head. Her heart beat in fear. She didn't want to die. She didn't want to drown. But her fears did not matter now. There were things that needed to be done. People they needed to help.

Lucius pulled on his clothes and limped on his half-shifted feet after her as they ran out of the home. As they dried, he was able to pick up the pace. The palace halls were filled with noise. They heard shouts and Lucius ran toward them.

"Stay close to me, boys," Bridget ordered her sons. They whimpered in response.

"This way," Rigel called out, waving his arms at a gathering crowd. She recognized a few people from town.

"The king," someone said, seeing Lucius. The words were repeated throughout the hall. "The king. The king. King Lucius."

All eyes turned to him, so trusting and willing to

follow his lead. He looked at them, and she knew the weight sitting on his shoulders. When he didn't speak, she joined him and took his hand.

"Lady Bridget has found a way for the Merr to breathe on the surface," Lucius said.

Bridget's eyes widened as all eyes turned to *her*. "Uh, yes, we have reason to believe that ingesting seaweed—"

"It works," Olivette stated loudly. "I saw the king breathe the surface air and live. As you may have felt, the dome is caving in, but you have survived the ending of a world before and you can do it again. Follow your king as he leads you back to the surface."

Murmurings of doubt and fear sounded.

Lucius nodded at her in thanks. "Listen to my wife—your queen."

The tremors started again. Screams filled the halls. Olivette barely registered the fact that he'd made the announcement that officially married them. This was hardly the wedding of a girl's dreams.

"Get to the surfacing area," Lucius ordered. "Everyone to the ocean. Stay with the hunters."

Lucius waved Brutus to his side. "Put hunters in the ocean. Swim them in groups away from the dome. Try to keep them calm. We'll have to feed them the seaweed in the water. This is a full-scale evacuation."

Lucius turned toward her and held her hands. "I need you to go to Crystal Cave and help keep people calm as they go into the ocean. I'll be there as soon as I can."

"Lucius..." She began to shake her head in denial and stopped. She didn't want to leave him. Not now. "I love you."

"And I you."

"Be safe," she whispered.

He leaned over and kissed her. "This is not our end. We'll find a way."

She hoped he was right.

Olivette nodded and went to do as he asked. She hurried through the hall, stopping beside Bridget to ask, "Will you and the boys come with me to the surfacing area? I need your help."

Children were too important to her husband and these people. They needed to be as close to safety as possible, even if that safety was the cold darkness of the abyss.

THOUGH IT MUST HAVE BEEN hours and nearly a thousand people that they'd helped into the water, it felt like mere seconds. Some were calm. Others cried. Still others tried to refuse. Many had not been in the water for hundreds of years. In the end, they all ended up in the water.

The dome continued to shift and move. Olivette turned to Bridget. Her sons were already in the water with their father. "It's time. You should go in the water with your family. You can answer everyone's questions from out there."

"What about you?" Bridget asked.

Olivette waved a woman into the cave. She carried a giant bundle in her arms. "This way. Ladies Lyra and Victoria will be waiting to guide you on the other side. Follow the tail in front of you and stay with the group. Everything will be all right. The king has a plan."

Bridget grabbed her arm and insisted, "What about you?"

She looked at the door, hoping as she did each time that the next person to come through would be her husband. "I can't leave yet."

Cassandra joined them. "That's almost everyone from the palace. The hunters are searching for stragglers."

"You should go with Bridget into the water. See if Lyra and Victoria need help," Olivette said.

"Where are we going to take all of them?" Cassandra asked. "Do we think the surface world is ready for an invasion of merfolk?"

"Lyra knows of a few places. She said her father and brothers would help relocate us. I have friends along the Washington coastline," Bridget said. "We might have to split up the population, but we'll think of something."

"There are several islands in the Caribbean that have no population," Cassandra suggested.

A man and two women entered the caves.

"We'll figure it out," Olivette said. To the newcomers, she gestured to the water. "Follow Ladies Bridget and Cassandra. They'll show you where to go."

15

LUCIUS FELT the emptiness of the dome as he looked up at the falling sky. Water poured in like a waterfall to fill the valley below. It swallowed the town, flooding the streets and the houses, erasing centuries in a few short seconds. Part of his heart broke in that moment as he watched the end of the world for the second time in his long life. He listened to make sure he could hear none of his people still trapped within.

"Lucius!"

He turned at the panicked sound of Olivette's voice. She ran out of the front gates of the palace toward him.

"What are you doing here? Why aren't you in the surfacing area?" he demanded.

Her eyes rounded as she took in the sight of the

dying world. "Wow. That's... This is really happening."

He kissed her and held her close. The anxious thud of her heart beat hard against his chest. He felt her fear and how hard she was trying to hide it.

"We are the only two left," he said. "Hrafn and Cain led people out through those tunnels we found in the countryside."

A loud crack sounded as the dome broke apart. Pieces of the shell dropped in a rush of water. A wave flowed forward from the town, lapping up at them from the palace gates.

"It's time." Lucius grabbed her arm and ran with her through the palace. The walls cracked around them, stones falling as the dome shifted under the new pressure of the ocean flood.

They ran toward the surfacing area. The ceiling cracked, falling in chunks to block the entrance to the Crystal Caves.

"How are we going to get out?" Olivette asked. She'd somehow managed to stay calm until that moment. She ran toward the rocks and tried to pull them. Lucius managed to slide one, but the entrance was too blocked.

'My king?' Demon's voice called from within the water.

'*The way is blocked. We'll meet you on the other side,*' he answered. '*You have my wishes if I don't make it.*'

"What did they say?" Olivette demanded. "I know that mind link look you get."

"We have to go out the other way," he said.

"What other way?"

He looked up.

"Shit," she whispered. "I'm scared, Lucius. I don't want to drown."

"I won't leave your side. I promise. Just hold on to me." He hated her fear but knew he had to get her to safety. He ran with her back out of the palace. The water had risen to the gates.

"Don't let go," she begged as he took her to the water's edge.

"Don't try to resist. Gulp as much water as you can into your lungs. It will be over soon." He wrapped his arms around her and kissed her.

Before she could pull away, he leapt backward, diving with her in his arms into the cold ocean water flooding his world. The currents carried him and he transformed. He swam with all his might while trying to hold on to his wife. She thrashed in his arms as he expected she would. Her eyes met his and he saw she held her breath.

'*I love you,*' he told her, hoping she'd hear.

Olivette's lips parted to release bubbles. She closed her eyes tight and breathed in.

As the water filled her lungs, she squirmed anew.

He wished he could take her pain, but all he could do was hold on tight as he swam them through the street. The current pushed them toward the mermaid statue before he was able to propel them upward to the top of the dome. Fish passed him, carried by the water. He dodged a squid on its way down.

Olivette stilled in his arms. He fought with all his might against the rush of water as it tried to toss him back and forth.

Suddenly, he felt the flicker of a tail against his.

His wife's eyes met his once more, and she wrapped her arms around his neck as she helped push them up with her tail. Lucius swept his arms for greater control. Together they made it to the top of the dome. His hand touched glass as the currents churned beneath them. He pulled them toward the crack and held on. He waited a few moments as the burning in his muscles subsided.

Olivette reached up, and they pulled their bodies out of Atlantes.

The water vibrated with the fear of his people.

Lucius followed the sensation, pulling his wife behind him.

'*Stop*,' Olivette said, her voice faint.

He obeyed, turning to see her. '*What is it?*'

She pointed behind them. The dome's light was fading into darkness.

'*We have to join the others*,' he said. '*We'll be safer in numbers.*'

'*I hear them*,' she said. '*So many voices.*'

'*And they hear you*,' he warned. '*Until you learn to control it.*'

'*I love you, Lucius. Forever.*' She squeezed his hand.

As they swam to join the others and lead his people up toward the surface, he didn't let go of her once. He was proud to have her by his side, his queen.

The hunters were already passing out seaweed rations and ordering more picked. Demon and Brutus hurried toward them as the news of their survival rang throughout the abyss.

16

EPILOGUE

TWO YEARS LATER...

Olivette sat on the shore watching the water for signs of her husband. The choppy water didn't worry her as it hit the beach. He led the others on an expedition for the special seaweed they needed to keep in their diet, like a multivitamin to be taken once a month to stop from feeling sick in the surface world. It was found in deep ocean, but they hoped to farm it closer to home.

Life was much different here than in Florida, but it felt safer for the Merr people as they settled into isolation. Not everyone stayed with the group. There were those who'd wandered off to different parts of the globe, some as far north as Nova Scotia and the coasts of Scotland. Others chose to settle uninhabited islands in the Caribbean. Most stayed near Olivette and her husband along the rocky Washington coast.

The ocean called to her like a siren's song, urging her to dive beneath the waves. She resisted with relative ease. The pull to swim was especially strong during the full moon. She closed her eyes and breathed deeply. He should be home soon. She felt him nearing the shore.

'*Is it safe?*'

She smiled, hearing Lucius in her head.

'*Yes, my love,*' she answered. '*I walked the coastline. No surprises.*'

Moments later she saw a man surface, then another, and another, until nearly twenty Merr appeared from beneath the waves. They navigated the shallow waters onto the rocky shoreline, crawling with their hands. Dark mesh bags hung over their backs, filled with the precious seaweed. The bright colors of their many tails decorated the brown rocks for a few moments before fins disappeared and scales turned to flesh. Several of the naked men nodded in her direction as she stood and carried two large beach bags toward them. She set them on the ground and began handing out towels. The mermen thanked her before moving to disappear into the trees, heading home.

"Thank you, my queen." Brutus winked as he took the towel. "Any word from my brothers about the hunt?"

"Two more scylla have been brought out of the waters and they went back to track a third," she said. "They're being rehabilitated near the old lighthouse. Bridget said they're growing stronger and showing no signs of translucence. Victoria is there helping out."

Brutus grinned, wiping his face with the towel. The black scales near his eyes disappeared. "These are truly blessed times."

"Tell your wife and brothers that we will have dinner at our house on Sunday," Olivette insisted, as he continued up the shore. "Lyra's brothers are visiting, and she wishes for us all to make them welcome. Iason and Cassandra are also swimming up from the Caribbean next week, too, to let us know how the settlement there is doing."

"Aye, my queen." Brutus lifted his hand in an acknowledgment without turning around. "We'll be there."

As always, Lucius was the last out of the water. He liked to make sure everyone made it home safely. She reached into the bag and took the last towel. She carried it toward him, careful not to step in the saltwater. He crawled on his hands up the rocky shore before turning around and brushing the water from his tail with his fingers. The sunlight glistened on his beautiful scales, highlighting the threads of pearl within. The transformation from Merr to human still fascinated her, even after two years.

"Welcome back, my love," she said, as he stood.

Instead of taking the towel, he wrapped his arms around her and dried his body by pressing against her. He kissed her softly. "You look beautiful."

Olivette giggled, not caring that he got her wet. Her legs tingled at the dampness but she didn't shift. "How was your swim?"

"I'm more concerned about you." His smile dropped. "What happened? I felt something while I was away."

Olivette pulled out of his arms so he could dry off properly and went back to the beach bags. She reached inside to pull out a printout she'd made from an online paper. She handed it to her husband. "They've arrested him."

"Him?" Lucius frowned as he looked at Tanner Tapert's picture. The blue scales around his eyes had not fully disappeared, and they darkened in his aggravation. The former senator's aide wore hand-cuffs as he was being led through a line of reporters.

Lucius stiffened, instantly growing angry. "Oh. Him."

"Those anonymous letters I wrote apparently sparked an investigation. They have quotes from some of the women on the boat about how he was manhandling them the night I was thrown over. Others came forward, and now at least a dozen rape victims are speaking out. They've taken his passport so he can't leave the country as he awaits trial."

"This is a good thing. Why are you upset?" He dropped the news article in the bag and pulled her into his arms. The sound of water crashing on rocks surrounded them as she thought about it.

Finally, she said, "I feel like I should have done more. There are so many women who have been hurt by him."

"Oh, my darling queen, you have done much. You drew their attention to him and made them look into his actions. And you protected the thousands of your Merr subjects by not exposing yourself to surface scrutiny. You found us this place and helped us settle. The surface has changed so much. Had we been left on our own, we would not have survived. Cameras and internet? How could we have imagined such a thing? We would have been exposed the first week." He kissed her forehead. "You said it yourself.

If you came forward and claimed he threw you overboard in the middle of the ocean with no proof of it happening, no proof of rescue, no evidence, and the fact you were still alive, no one would believe you. They had to find the facts for themselves, and they have. He has been exposed for the monster he is."

"I know you're right. I should be content with the fact that justice is being done." She picked up the empty beach bags and hooked her arm through his. She led him up the shore toward the dirt path that would take them home. "I think I just needed to hear you say it. I'm too much in my own head when you're gone. I hate not being able to hear you in my thoughts."

'I am always within you, my love, even if you cannot hear me,' Lucius' voice whispered in her mind.

'I love you, my king, come what may, I will always love you,' she answered.

Lucius grinned and swept her into his arms. The towel slipped from his waist and fell onto the dirt path. He didn't bother to pick it up as he carried his wife home.

The End

THANK YOU, readers, for your love and support of the Merr. As they transition to the surface world, King Lucius has requested that if you happen to be looking out at the ocean and see something not fully human, please do not take pictures. They mean you no harm.

ABOUT MICHELLE M. PILLOW

New York Times & *USA TODAY*
Bestselling Author

Michelle loves to travel and try new things, whether it's a paranormal investigation of an old Vaudeville Theatre or climbing Mayan temples in Belize. She believes life is an adventure fueled by copious amounts of coffee.

Newly relocated to the American South, Michelle is involved in various film and documentary projects with her talented director husband. She is mom to a fantastic artist. And she's managed by a dog and cat who make sure she's meeting her deadlines.

For the most part she can be found wearing pajama pants and working in her office. There may or may not be dancing. It's all part of the creative process.

**Come say hello! Michelle loves talking
with readers on social media!**

www.MichellePillow.com

facebook.com/AuthorMichellePillow

twitter.com/michellepillow

instagram.com/michellempillow

bookbub.com/authors/michelle-m-pillow

goodreads.com/Michelle_Pillow

amazon.com/author/michellepillow

youtube.com/michellepillow

pinterest.com/michellepillow

COMPLIMENTARY EXCERPTS

LOVE POTIONS EXCERPT THE DRAGON'S QUEEN

BY MICHELLE M. PILLOW

Warlocks MacGregor® **Book 1**

Contemporary Paranormal Scottish Warlocks

A little magickal mischief never hurt anyone...

Erik MacGregor, from a clan of ancient Scottish warlocks, isn't looking for love. After centuries, it's not even a consideration...until he moves in next door to Lydia Barratt. It's clear that the shy beauty wants nothing to do with him, but he's drawn to her nonetheless and determined to win her over.

Lydia Barratt just wants to be left alone to grow flowers and make lotions in her old Victorian house. The last thing she needs is a demanding Scottish man meddling in her private life. Just because he's gorgeous and totally rocks a kilt doesn't mean she's going to fall for his seductive manner.

But Erik won't give up and just as Lydia let's her guard down, his sister decides to get involved. Her little love potion prank goes terribly wrong, making Lydia the target of his sudden embarrassingly obsessive behavior. They'll have to find a way to pull Erik out of the spell fast when it becomes clear that Lydia has more than a lovesick warlock to worry about. Evil lurks within the shadows and it plans to use Lydia, alive or dead, to take out Erik and his clan for good.

Love Potions Excerpt

"Ly-di-ah! I sit beneath your window, laaaass, singing 'cause I loooove your a—""

"For the love of St. Francis of Assisi, someone call a vet. There is an injured animal screaming in pain outside," Charlotte interrupted the flow of music in ill-humor.

Lydia lifted her forehead from the kitchen table. Her windows and doors were all locked, and yet Erik's endlessly verbose singing penetrated the barrier of glass and wood with ease.

Charlotte held her head and blinked heavily. Her red-rimmed eyes were filled with the all too poignant look of a hangover. She took a seat at the table and laid her head down. Her moan sounded something like, "I'm never moving again."

"You need fluids," Lydia prescribed, getting up to pour unsweetened herbal tea from the pitcher in the fridge. She'd mixed it especially for her friend. It was Gramma Annabelle's hangover recipe of willow bark, peppermint, carrot, and ginger. The old lady always had a fresh supply of it in the house while she was alive. Apparently, being a natural witch also meant in partaking in natural liquors. Annabelle had kept a steady supply of moonshine stashed in the basement. If the concert didn't stop soon she might try to find an old bottle.

"*Ly-di-ah!*"

"Omigod. Kill me," Charlotte moaned. "No. Kill him. Then kill me."

"*Ly-di-ah!*"

Erik had been singing for over an hour. At first, he'd tried to come inside. She'd not invited him and the barrier spell sent him sprawling back into the yard. He didn't seem to mind as he found a seat on some landscaping timbers and began his serenade. The last time she'd asked him to be quiet, he'd gotten louder and overly enthusiastic. In fact, she'd been too scared to pull back the curtains for a clearer look, but she was pretty sure he'd been dancing on her lawn, shaking his kilt.

"Omigod," Charlotte muttered, pushing up and angrily going to a window. Then grimacing, she said, "Is he wearing a tux jacket with his kilt?"

"Don't let him see you," Lydia cried out in a panic. It was too late. The song began with renewed force.

"He's..." Charlotte frowned. "I think it's dancing."

Since the damage was done, Lydia joined Charlotte at the window. Erik grinned. He lifted his arms to the side and kicked his legs, bouncing around the yard like a kid on too much sugar. "Maybe it's a traditional Scottish dance?"

Both women tilted their heads in unison as his kilt kicked up to show his perfectly formed ass.

"He's not wearing..." Charlotte began.

"I know. He doesn't," Lydia answered. Damn, the man had a fine body. Too bad Malina's trick had turned him insane.

To find out more about Michelle's books visit www.MichellePillow.com

THE SAVAGE KING EXCERPT

CAT-SHIFTER ROMANCE

by Michelle M. Pillow

Lords of the Var® Book One by Michelle M. Pillow

Bestselling Cat-shifter Romance Series

Cat-shifting King Kirill knows he must do his duty by his people. When his father unexpectedly dies, it's his destiny to take the throne and all of the responsibility that entails. What he hadn't prepared for is the troublesome prisoner that's now his to deal with.

Undercover Agent Ulyssa is no man's captive. Trapped in a primitive forest awaiting pickup, she's going to make the best out of a bad situation...which doesn't include falling for the seductions of a king.

About *Lords of the Var*® (Books 1-5)

You met their father, King Attor, in Dragon Lords Books 1-4, now meet the Var Princes!

The cat-shifter princes were raised to not believe in love, especially love for one woman, and they will do everything in their power to live up to their father's expectations. Oh, how the mighty will fall.

The Savage King Excerpt

Kirill watched the door to his bedroom open. He'd been sitting in the dark, trying to relieve the stress headache that had built behind his eyes for the last week. The pain started at the base of his skull and radiated up to his temples until he could hardly see straight.

A heavy responsibility had been thrust on his shoulders, a responsibility he really hadn't prepared himself for, the welfare of the Var people. King Attor had not left him in a good position. He'd rallied the people to the brink of war, convinced them that the

Draig were their enemy, and even went so far as to attack the Draig royal family.

Kirill wanted to see peace in the land. However, he knew the facts didn't bode well for it. The Draig had a long list of grievances against King Attor and the Var kingdom.

Before his death, the king had ordered an attack on the four Draig princes, all of which ended horribly for the Var. The worst was when Prince Yusef was stabbed in the back, a most cowardly embarrassment for the Var guard who did it. If he hadn't been executed in the Draig prisons, he would've been ostracized from the Var community. Luckily, Prince Yusef survived or they'd already be at battle.

Attor had also arranged for the kidnapping of Yusef's new bride. The Draig Princess Olena had been rescued, or that too would've led to war. The old king had even tried to poison Princess Morrigan, the future Draig queen, on two separate occasions. She too lived. And those were only a few of the offenses Kirill knew about in the few weeks before King Attor's death. He could just imagine what he didn't know.

Kirill sighed, feeling very tired. He'd known since birth that the day would come when he'd be expected to step up and lead the Var as their new king. He just hadn't expected it to be for another hundred or so years. His father had been a hard man, whom he'd foolishly believed was invincible.

"Here kitty, kitty, kitty." His lovely houseguest's whisper drew his complete attention from his heavy thoughts.

Ulyssa bent over like she expected him to answer to the insulting call. He dropped his fingers from his temple into his lap, and a quizzical smile came to his lips. As he watched her, he wasn't sure if he was angered or amused by her words.

"Are you in here, you little furball?" she said, a little louder.

She wore his clothes. Never had the outfit looked sexier. His jaw tightened in masculine interest, as he unabashedly looked her over. All too well did he remember the softness of her body against his and the gentle, offering pleasure of her sweet lips. She'd made soft whimpering noises when he'd touched her, yielding, purring sounds in the back of her throat. Even with the aid of nef, he was surprised by how easily and confidently she melted into him. The Var were wild, passionate people and were drawn to the same qualities in others. He suspected she'd be an untamed lover.

Too bad she'd belonged to his father first. In his mind, that made her completely untouchable though none would dare question his claim if he were to take her to his bed. Technically, by Var law, she belonged to him until he chose to release her. For an insane moment, he thought about keeping her as a lover. He knew he wouldn't, but the thought was entertaining.

Kirill's grin deepened. Ulyssa strode across his home to the bathroom door with an irritated scowl. It was obvious she didn't see him in the darkened corner, watching her. He detected her engaging smell from across the room, the smell of a woman's desire. It stirred his blood, making his limbs heavy with arousal. And, for the first time since his father's death, his headache relieved itself.

"Hum, maybe I'm looking too high. I'm sure there has to be a little cat door here somewhere. Come here, little kitty. Where are you hiding?"

His slight smile fell at her words. It was easy to detect her mocking tone.

"Where's your little kitty door, huh?" Ulyssa whispered to herself, her blue gaze searching around in the dark.

Kirill grimaced in further displeasure. He watched her open the door to his weapons cabinet. Her eyes rounded, and he thought she might take one. She didn't. Instead, she nodded in appreciation before closing the door and continuing her search for an exit.

She stopped at a narrow window by his kitchen doorway. Her neck craned to the side, as she tried to see out over the distance. Kirill knew she looked at the forest. From under her breath, he heard her vehement whisper, "Where exactly did you little fur balls bring me? Ugh, I need to get out of this flea trap, even if I have to fight every one of you cowardly felines to do it. I've fought species twice as big and three times as frightening. A couple of little kitty cats don't scare me."

If this insolent woman wanted to play tough, oh, he'd play. Curling gracefully forward, Kirill shifted before his hands even touched the ground. He let one thick paw land silently on the floor, followed by a second. Short black fur rippled over his tanned flesh, blending him into the shadows. His clothes fell from his body, and he lowered his head as he crept forward. A low sound of warning started in the back of his throat. He was livid.

To find out more about Michelle's books visit www.MichellePillow.com

PLEASE LEAVE A REVIEW
THANK YOU FOR READING!

Please take a moment to share your thoughts by reviewing this book.

Be sure to check out Michelle's other titles at www.MichellePillow.com